LAURA LUKASAVAGE

Will's Awakening

First edition

ISBN: 978-1-956994-05-6

Editing by Elaine Stephens
Editing by Astrid Aurelius

This book was professionally typeset on Reedsy.
Find out more at reedsy.com

This series is for my mother, my best friend. A relationship and connection that never faltered never crumbled, even in death it's as thick and strong as concrete. Her memory is what pushes me on to be the best person and mother I can be and to follow my dreams. Taken too soon but never forgotten. You are with me every day. I miss you, love you to the moon and back.

Something waits deep inside the darkness of
my mind,
Revealing the truths that have kept me blind.
With loss comes truth,
Waiting to shatter my youth.
He hungers to be free,
Learning now that I am the key.
Will I be strong enough to fight the darkness?
Only with my newfound truth that I must
harness.
Embrace the light and remember where you
come from,
To the darkness you must not succumb.
Your destiny awaits.
Are you their savor or their doom?
Your hands hold everyone's fate.

-LAURA LUKASAVAGE

Contents

Acknowledgement

I want to say a special thank you to two amazing women who helped make this book what it is today. Without your advice, editing and words of encouragement it would have been a lot longer before this book saw the light of day. Thank you to fellow Indie author Astrid Aurelius who has five wonderful books of her own on Amazon, go check them out. You can catch her on Instagram @astridaurelius. Thank you for reading and reviewing and being a friend. I also want to thank Elaine Stephens, who can be found on Instagram @elaine_stephens_reviews. Thank you for being a constant. Always there to listen and give advice and keep me going. Thank you for all the hours of editing, reading, reviewing and YouTube videos you have done for me. I appreciate everything you both do.

Lastly, thank you to all my readers, reviewers and followers for without you this dream of mine would be nothing. I really hope you enjoy this book and the future ones to come.

Laura's Other Works

Chapter 1

Something sinister and impure lurks in the darkness, awakening a deep feeling in my bones that I can't ignore. Whatever's out there, hiding in the night, it's hunting me and I'm a sitting duck waiting to be devoured by the predator.

A breeze caresses the back of my neck, sending chills running through my body. I inhale slowly and deeply, trying to calm my breathing. I can feel the darkness creeping closer and with it, this savage entity.

I want to stare this nightmare in the face, sending it running in the other direction. Have it curl into a ball at my feet and cower in fear. I want it to know what it feels like to be in my shoes. To feel like there's no escape, no safe place to hide. I'm unarmed, alone and in the dark, and whatever is out there watching me already has the upper hand.

It can see me.

Ignoring my crippling fear and the voice screaming in my head to run, I turn away from the shadows taking a step in the opposite direction hoping that whatever it is will either leave or finally come out of the night and show itself.

"I can sense your fear, boy."

My eyes scan over the forest but the thing that calls to me is nowhere in sight. But the fear in my chest calms because now at least I know one thing. What I'm facing isn't an animal, it's human. At least now I stand a chance of getting out of here alive.

The air around me shifts, caressing my shoulders as it passes by.

"Why do you fear me?" The deep male voice asks from the shadows.

I remain silent. After all, someone who lurks in the shadows can only mean trouble.

"I'm not going anywhere." He whispers in my ear, causing me to tremble.

I turn around fast but the owner of the voice is nowhere in sight.

"I wish to converse with you."

Before I can stop myself the words come rushing out, "You could just say talk. No need to sound so proper. What were you born in the thirty's or something?"

A sinister laugh breaks through the shadows behind me, causing a shiver to run down my spine.

"So, you do have a backbone?"

I sigh, trying to gain my composure as I stand up straight. There's no going back now, mine as well find out why this person is following me and why from the shadows. "What do you want?"

"I thought I made that clear?"

"You said you want to talk but, talk about what?"

His voice moving closer, he replies, "You are the one I've been looking for."

This guys making no sense. "Meaning?"

"You are the chosen one."

I try to keep the annoyance from my tone but I fail miserably, "Chosen for what?"

His following words come right above my left ear. "You are the one who will release me from this place."

My gaze moves upwards to once again find no one there. "Release you?"

"Maybe the better term is awaken me but since I am confined here with no way out, other than you, I figured saying you will release me was more adequate."

I shake my head, trying to make sense of the gibberish that continues to come from his mouth. "What are you talking about?"

"OK, maybe this one will make more sense to you. You are my meat suit."

I laugh uncomfortably. "I don't know what you're talking about, but it's time for me to wake up now."

I lift my right hand to my left forearm and pinch myself lightly.

Nothing.

I pinch harder until my eyes squint and my teeth bare down on one another.

"This has to be a dream. I need to wake up." I mumble to myself.

This can't be real, this whole situation is down right insane.

"You'll wake up when I let you."

Trying to drown out his creepy voice, I close my eyes. I need to wake up and get away from this insane dream and return to the nightmare my life has become.

"You will free me; they will find you."

"Who?"

"My followers. They are closing in on you, Will."

The way he says my name sends a chill through my body.

How does he know my name?

What kind of dream is this?

I want to wake up now.

"This is more than a mere dream."

"Yeah, it's a nightmare," I mumble.

He laughs disturbingly. "No, this isn't a nightmare, dear boy. This is your future calling."

"Will? Will, wake up."

I hear a woman's voice calling to me from somewhere far away. I strain trying to focus on it, but I can't. The man says something else to me, but my ears feel waterlogged as his voice moves into the background and the woman's draws closer. So I try to focus on it. It sounds so familiar.

I know her.

I listen harder.

It's my mother. She's calling out to me from somewhere far away.

Suddenly I'm being shaken. She's trying to rouse my sleeping body. I focus harder. I want to wake up. I need to wake up.

The entity in the darkness draws closer, causing the air around me to become unbearably cold. I wrap my arms around myself, begging to wake up. His darkness is overpowering as evil fills the gap between us.

My body feels like a ton of rocks.

"You think I'm going to let you leave?" He laughs in a sinister manner. "You're my way out of this hell hole. With you, I will live again. I've waited over a hundred years for you to come and release me from this place, from my torment."

I feel the emptiness inside me growing the closer he gets. I'm losing myself, becoming something, someone else. He's doing something to me, and as hard as I fight, it makes no difference. I fall to my knees as the crippling hollowness inside my chest grows, and he laughs in the darkness around me.

My mother's cool hands shaking my body pull me from the dark. I focus on them and nothing else. I think of her kind but now, sad eyes. Her beautiful thick hair in a bun neatly on top of her head. I think about how much she needs me now, how much we need each other, and suddenly I'm weightless.

My body becomes transparent as my form turns to nothingness. I feel as light as air and moments later I'm falling through the earth.

The darkness yelling at me from above, "You'll never be free of me. You'll never be safe. I will find you! You will set me free!"

Then nothing.

The voice and hollowness are gone, and I can breathe once more. My eyelids stuck together with sleep, I use my heavy hands, weighted down from exhaustion, to feel around the surface underneath my body. The object is nice and cold to the touch, comforting. It's some kind of fabric.

Cotton.

A smile creeps over my face when I realize I'm in my bed. I'm no longer stuck in my dream, no longer surrounded by the darkness. I work harder to peel my eyelids apart. Once I get them open, they fall on my mother sitting on my bed next to me.

"You were having a bad dream."

I focus on her shape as my eyes readjust to the room. She's wearing the elegant aqua dress that hangs just off her shoulders. It's the one my brother, West, got for her before...

Moving to prop myself up on my elbows I whisper, "I'm sorry."

She smiles at me reassuringly. "They seem to be becoming a regular thing again."

I sigh, "Yeah."

"What was it about this time?"

I turn my attention to the open window, not wanting to think about the emptiness I couldn't escape only moments ago.

My mother breathes in deep, "You don't need to tell me. I just wish you would talk to someone about them."

"I can't," I whisper.

"I don't understand what's so bad about them that you won't talk to someone."

"They're... dark and disturbing, and I don't want to be psychoanalyzed or medicated."

My mother's lime green eyes hold a mountain of sadness as she looks down at me. "I wouldn't let that happen."

"If I go and talk with someone about my dreams and about what's been going on in my life, they will think I need help."

She sighs. "You have been through something traumatic, Will. No one will think less of you because of how things have turned out since."

I gaze at her with envy, "You went through the same thing, yet you can function. So why can't I?"

"I may look like I'm functioning on the outside, but on the inside." She stops abruptly.

I place my hand on hers silently as my eyes land on the clock, seeing it reads 8:34 p.m.

"What time did I go to bed?"

"Don't ask me. I wasn't here, remember?" Her smile reaches her eyes.

She stands, making her way to my bedroom door. The place where she was sitting only moments ago still holds her shape. I look down at it as it starts to rise, and her impression disappears.

She lingers in the doorway, looking at me as her smile fades. "Are you OK, Will?"

With a lot of effort, I peel my eyes away from the spot on the bed and look over to where my mother is now standing.

I look into her weary eyes and smile. "I'm fine. Just dealing with the aftermath of another bad dream." I shrug, "You know, the usual."

She lifts her thin, frail arms to rest her hands on opposite sides of the threshold before tilting her head sideways as she looks at me, then sliding her hands down the woodwork until they come to meet together once more.

Her eyes looking into my soul. Her dyed auburn hair resting at her shoulders, like usual, unless she's working, then it's pulled up into a tight bun on top of her head. She works at a nearby hospital as a nurse. She used to love the job, but I can tell she doesn't care for it much anymore. I see how worn down she has become, part of it from all the hours she works, and the other because of what happened.

My mind drifts as fear seeps back into my thoughts, and I begin to wonder if she still blames me for what happened.

"Mom?"

"Yes?"

"I'm sorry."

Her eyes widen with uncertainty. "Sorry? For what?"

Turning away, my gaze falls on my old beat-up gray hoodie, and the memory of the day my brother bought it for me creeps into my mind. "You know what."

She moves away from the door, taking a step towards me but stops herself from taking another. "Will, stop that."

I flip my head around to look at her, anger rising. "Stop what? Stop saying I'm sorry? Well, I can't, Mom, because I am. If it wasn't for me, I may not remember what happened, but one thing I know for sure is it was my fault."

She sits down next to me again, laying her left hand on mine. It's so cold I almost pull my hand back. The diamond ring my father got her for their wedding day comes into my line of sight, and I'm mad all over again.

"Why are you still wearing that?" I ask as I throw my chin toward the object in question.

She looks down at the ring. "Because I still love your father no matter what happened." Her eyes finding mine, she continues, "And I still love you. I don't blame you, and it's time for you to stop blaming yourself."

"Well, that's not going to happen anytime soon."

"I know things have been hard on you, and I'm sorry. We should have talked about what happened, but I didn't know how to."

A smile creeps up on my face as I look at her. "Who's blaming who now?"

"You always know what to say." She chuckles lightly.

I wonder what she means, but decide not to ask. Instead, I ask a different question, "Why did Dad leave? Like, the real reason."

The smile is ripped from her face so fast that my heart stops.

"He couldn't handle it, I suppose."

Her hand pats mine as a river begins forming in her eyes. She says I always know the right things to say, but it seems I know all the wrong things, too. She wraps her fingers lightly around my wrist as she moves into a standing position.

"Come out with me and get something to eat."

"I already ate."

She stares at me for a moment before smiling. "No, you didn't. Now, come on."

Being a small woman of only 5'4, she sure does have some muscles, I think as she yanks me off my warm bed and into the cool night air running through the rest of the house. Taking in her appearance fully, a question forms in my mind, one I'm afraid I might not like the answer to.

"Mom?"

She looks over her shoulder at me but keeps walking. "Yes?"

"Where were you?"

Her cheeks turn a dark crimson as she turns forward. "I changed after work and went out for a drink with a few friends I work with."

"Who?"

"Just friends."

Starting to feel like the parent, I say, "You never dress like that."

"What, I can't dress up nice once in a while without getting a lecture from my son?"

I smile and nod, but say nothing.

"Well, too bad, mister, because sometimes even a mother likes to dress up and go out on the town and feel beautiful for a night," She says with a smirk.

"But mom," I pause as she stops and turns toward me, "you always look beautiful. You don't need to dress up for that."

Tears start to form in her eyes again before she pulls me in for an embrace and whispers, "Thank you, honey. Sometimes, it's nice to hear."

I smile into her shoulder, hugging her back, thankful that we still have each other and always will.

* * *

I open my eyes as sweat runs down my face. I take notice of the midnight blue paint splatter on the ceiling as the memory moves to the front of my mind.

My older brother, West, wanted to toss the football around, and I wanted to finish my ocean painting. West became impatient and playfully took the brush out of my hand. He did it with such force that the blue paint I had just applied to it spread across the ceiling. So we looked at one another and erupted into laughter.

I close my eyes, releasing a long breath.

This isn't the first time I've had this dream. It seems to resurface at least once a week since it happened almost four months ago. The man in the darkness is still a mystery to me, but I know for sure that I don't ever want to experience what I did in that dream again.

A lot has changed in my life this last year. My brother's death and father's absence were only the beginning of my life turning upside down. Christmas break is almost over, and soon it will be time to face the destruction my life has become. One thing I am excited about is getting back to school. At least one thing hasn't changed.

Chapter 2

"When does school start?" My mother's voice rings through the house to my still sleepy body.

"I think it's the 10th of January."

"Isn't that this coming week?"

I smile at my bowl of Cheerios that are beginning to turn soggy. "Aren't you a smart one?"

I turn to see her entering the kitchen as she puts her stud butterfly earring in her left ear. Yet again, something my brother gave to her.

"Don't sass me," she replies.

"I can't help it. You always set yourself up for it. Plus, it's my job as your son to sass you." I flash her a playful smile.

"You don't need to do anything, young man, except get up every morning and go to school."

I return my spoon to its milky grave. "OK, so I guess I don't have to do the shopping, or take out the trash, or watch any more of those awful romance movies with you anymore, or-"

Lifting her hands, she closes her eyes, saying, "Now hold on there one minute. I'm sorry, I forgot to add those things to the list. You will continue to go shopping and take out the trash and all the other things, too. But most of all, you will continue to watch those 'awful' movies as you call them, and you will enjoy every minute." A smile spreads across her make-up-covered, young-looking face, her eyes falling to my half-eaten bowl of cereal. "And make sure you eat all of that."

I turn my attention back to my cereal. "I will."

"I'm sure," she says with a giggle.

It's funny to look at your mom as a friend, but that's what mine is. She's my best friend, always has been, and I'm happy that hasn't changed. Being only nineteen years older, I guess it's easier for us to relate and get along better than most kids do with their parents. My mom and dad got married when she was sixteen, and then she got pregnant with my brother before she was seventeen, and then got pregnant again with me when she was eighteen. She is now the ripe age of thirty-seven.

"What are your plans today?"

I move my spoon around in the bowl before I answer. "Honestly, I couldn't tell you."

"Why don't you give Trey a call?"

I put my spoon, which is now full of Cheerios, into my mouth. "Because we haven't talked in months." I sputter through a mouthful of cereal.

Mom's face scrunches up as she looks away. "I hate it when you do that."

"Do what?" I slur.

"Talk with food in your mouth," she replies in a stern voice.

I smile as I put the spoon to my lips and add more cereal to my mouth before turning to her, "Is this better?" I choke out.

I make the Cheerios visible from in-between my gapped teeth.

"Ew, Will. Really? Ugh, fine, do what you want. Just promise me you won't sit in the house by yourself all day."

I nod as she makes her way to the front door and grabs her coat off the coat holder, adding it to her morning attire.

I swallow my mouthful of cereal and call out to her before she gets through the threshold, "Love you, Mom. Have a good day."

She stops, poking her head back in the door to smile at me. "I love you too. See you tonight."

* * *

My hand rests on the rusty old copper doorknob as my body refuses to make a move to open the door. I know who's on the other side, and I don't feel like being bothered, not today. Trey Jefferson used to be my best friend, but like everything else in my life this past year, that's now a thing of the past. It's like we never knew each other. I don't know if it's because of his new status at school, mister big shot quarterback, or if it's because of the deeper, body-paralyzing reason.

Trey became one of the most famous people in school almost overnight, and let's face it, being in high school, you can't have a nobody as a best friend when everyone knows your name. It just wouldn't be feasible. His rise to fame came on fast, and, being a Sophomore, it was perfect. So we kept in touch until summertime, and then Junior year began when tragedy struck not once, but twice.

Being Junior year, we both knew it was time to focus on what would grab a college's attention, and Trey being the quarterback of our football team was a step in the right direction. So, I took a step back. OK, I'm not being entirely honest. Part of this might be my fault. After what happened, I didn't want to be around anyone, not even myself, so I didn't put up the fight I should have when Trey placed me on the bench. Nothing mattered to me anymore. Not school, college applications, not even my friends.

Anger rears its ugly head at the thought of Trey, my father, and my brother, and it takes every bit of strength I have to push it back down.

Way down.

Into the emptiness that has become a part of me.

I close my eyes, releasing a long-repressed sigh. I haven't seen Trey since school ended for Christmas break a little over a month ago. I open my eyes, and they travel the length of the door till they land on my hand as I turn the knob slowly until I hear it click. I pull the door towards me, and Trey comes into view, standing on the front step.

The last time I looked at Trey, his sandy blonde hair was a buzz cut, but today it's the longest I've ever seen, dangling just below the bottom of his ears. The only thing about him that's left unchanged is his height. Being 6'2, he looms over me by two inches. Might not seem like a big height difference but I guess when it comes to us guys height is the first thing we measure up against. His coffee-color eyes find my sapphire ones when he turns in my direction.

"Hey," he mumbles while trying to force a smile.

"What's up?"

"Can I come in?"

I open the door wider and reluctantly move to the side, out of his way. "Sure."

Trey walks into the living room. As he walks past me, I swear I smell cigarette smoke on his flannel top. It seems more than just his hair and dress code has changed.

Trey approaches the couch hesitantly, turning around to face me. "How was your holiday?"

I fold my arms over my chest. "It was OK. I haven't been doing much. How about you?"

"The family and I went on a vacation, like every year. Nothing special."

"Cool."

Trey shoves his hands inside the pockets of his faded jeans. "So, how's your mom been dealing with everything?"

How do you think she's doing?

"She's fine, thanks for asking," I say sarcastically.

Trey looks away and out the front window to our lawn before speaking again. "And how about you? How are you doing?"

I hesitate for a moment. "I'm fine."

I'm tired of the small talk. That's how I'm doing.

Trey turns back around to face me with a knowing expression on his face. "You know you can talk to me."

I stick my chin up as I straighten my body to stand erect. "I said I'm fine."

Trey smiles, shaking his head as he runs his hand through the hair on the back of his head. "You forget we grew up together. I know you almost better than you know yourself, and no one in their right mind would be OK after what happened." His eyes turn sad before he continues, "You've always been strong, Will, but you're not that strong. No one is."

I throw my hands up in the air and turn away from him. "You caught me.

I'm a bloody wreck." I turn on him hard, daggers for eyes, "But you're the last person I want to talk about my feelings to."

"Listen, I'm not trying to make you mad, I just…I wanted to make sure you're doing OK."

"Yeah, now! What about for the last few months? Where were you then?"

"Look, I'm sorry. I know I haven't been a best friend to you lately, but I don't know how to be anymore. I don't know what to say or not say around you."

"I'm sorry it's so hard."

The hostility in my tone causes his eyes to widen.

Trey releases a long breath. "I didn't come here to argue."

"Then why did you come?"

"Because I care about you. You're my best friend, and I should have been there for you more than I was. I'm hoping I can change that now."

"How?"

"I don't know. I was hoping we could start over. Thea and I are going out with some friends to a party tonight before school starts back up. You should come."

Thea.

His sister.

Averting my gaze from him I mumble, "I'll think about it."

"Don't say that if you don't mean it."

"Fine."

Turning his back towards me, he whispers, "I should get going. I have to get ready for the party."

Trey walks over to the front door and closes his right hand over the copper knob. "I am sorry, and I hope we can move past these last few months. I don't want to throw our lifelong friendship down the drain because of a moment of stupidity on my part."

He turns away once more, opens the door, and lets in the cool, mid-afternoon air. I stifle a shiver as Trey closes the door behind him. The last thing I see is his back.

* * *

It's been hours since Trey left, and I've thought about going to the party a million times since then. The text message telling me where the party is only made me think about going that much more. But, I'm not ready.

More than that.

They aren't ready.

I'm not in the in-crowd. I'm not popular. Going would only make my already hard life more unbearable, giving me a taste of something I never cared to have and then taking it away in the morning. Where Trey is found on the football field, I can be found in the art room painting or drawing away, getting lost in the easy strokes of the brush or pencil in my hands, watching my vision unfold before my eyes. That is where I find my peace. Well, there and, for some odd reason, learning and studying. I've always been the brain, well, Thea and I both. Trey and West never cared much for school and studies, so when Thea and I would be preparing for the next test, they could be found outside throwing around the football.

So, the thought of going to a party with a bunch of jocks when I'm considered the nerd and rejected, no, I think I'll pass. My life is already twisted up enough without adding a few more jerks and their cruel words to the mix.

My mom should be home soon anyway, and I've made it a ritual to be home when she gets in from work. I'm not too fond of the idea of her coming home to a dark, quiet house. We are already more than aware of what is missing, what we've lost. It's there every day. I don't want to add to that emptiness for her, so I will continue to be here where I'm needed.

I make her a plate of dinner consisting of boneless chicken, mac and cheese, and corn. After making my way over to the living room couch and flopping down on it, I pick up the remote and aim it at the 60' flat-screen. The TV changes from pitch black to a light blue before the picture pops up on the screen. I only look at it for a second before I hear a knock on the front door. I close my eyes, throwing my head back against the soft brown couch. I know it's Trey, and he's going to try to get me to come to the party, so I choose to ignore the annoying noise in the background.

The knocking continues.

I sigh as I push myself up off the couch and stomp over to the front door. "I'm coming."

I pull the door wide open, ready to flip out when my eyes connect with deep brown ones and hair the color of the sun.

Thea.

"What are you doing here?"

That smile.

A few years ago, my brother had bluntly pointed out to me how Thea and I would make the perfect couple. He would always tell me how he would catch her watching me when I wasn't paying attention and when I would act like it wasn't a big deal, he would enlighten me, saying, "Bro, it's a pretty big deal." He told me he could tell she had feelings for me, but I would always brush them under the rug because my friendship with her and her brother was more important than dating her. Then, there is the underlying reason. I'm not good enough for her. Thea is the smartest in our class, beautiful and kind. All in all, she's the best person I know, right up there with my mom. If I could ever see myself with someone, it would be her for so many reasons I can't even mention. She's everything you would want in a friend, girlfriend, or person in your life in general.

"Sorry to show up without warning; Trey was going to text you, but I told him not to."

"Why?"

"Because I knew you would tell him to tell me not to come."

The way she's looking at me makes me feel like someone really sees me for the first time in a long time, sees how broken and messed up I've become, and suddenly I feel very exposed.

I look away from her as a smile creeps up on my face. "You're right."

"Of course I am."

I glance back at her to find her face mimics my own. "Would you like to come in?"

"Yes, please."

I move out of the way, allowing her to enter the TV-lit room. She slowly walks past me while never removing her eyes from mine. I'm the first to look away. I close the door quietly behind her as she makes her way to the living room.

"How are your dreams?"

I'm taken aback by the question. "What do you mean?"

"The last time we spoke, you said you had weird, and sometimes bad dreams."

"Oh, yeah." I throw my hand behind my head to rub my neck.

"Well, they are better, I hope."

"Yes." I lie.

Thea looks away from me, the smile never leaving her face. "You're lying."

"What is it with you and your brother telling me I'm lying?"

She stops short with her finger circling the top of the flower lamp closest to her. "Am I wrong?"

Defeated, I sigh, "No."

"I didn't think so." Her smile widens until it reaches her eyes.

The front door opens, and we both turn to see my mother walk in.

"Will, I'm home."

Her eyes come to rest on Thea, who looks at her with a smile, and my mother smiles back.

"Thea?" My mother whispers.

"Hello, Mrs. Walker."

"Thea, I told you before, call me Teresa. Mrs. Walker is so formal, and you've known Will since he was in diapers."

I groan at her comment, but she ignores me, continuing.

"I was hoping by now you would have thought of me more like a second mother."

Thea smiles. "I'm sorry." She glances over in my direction, "it's been a long time, too long." She turns her attention back to my mother. "But yes, I've always considered you like a second mother. I've missed coming here."

"Good." My mother makes her way over to us and takes Thea in her arms. "And yes, it has been a long time since I've last seen you. We've missed having

16

you around." She pulls back to look at Thea as her hands come to rest on her elbows. "How is everyone?"

"Very well, thank you."

They release each other, and my mom looks at me before walking into the kitchen.

I call to her, "I made you a plate. It's in the fridge."

She turns around to look at me. "Thank you." Looking at Thea, she nudges her chin in my direction, "isn't he the best?"

Thea giggles. "Yes, yes, he is."

My cheeks burn as I look at Thea, unsure of what to say next. "So."

She turns her attention to me. "So."

We look at each other in uncomfortable silence before she breaks it. "Your dreams."

Surprised, I ask. "What about them?"

"I know you were lying before."

"So, what if I was?"

She sighs. "I know it's been a while, Will, but you could always talk to me before. Please, don't close me out now. I'm trying."

"There's nothing to say." I turn my back to her, heading back to the couch. Other than my dreams have taken an even creepier turn.

I feel her eyes burning a hole through me as I sit on the couch. She makes her way across the room and back to my side.

"Will."

I look up at her, but say nothing.

She sits next to me placing a hand on mine. "I know you well enough to know something is going on. Something is bothering you,something more than West."

We sit in silence for a moment at the mention of my brother's name before I break the silence.

"And if I said I didn't want to talk about it?"

She sighs. "Then I guess I would have to respect that, as much as I don't want to."

"Thank you."

"But if you ever change your mind and need someone to listen…"

"I know."

"Good." Pausing, she stands, "I should be going. But promise me when we go back to school, we won't be strangers."

I smile after her as she moves towards the front door. "I promise."

To my surprise I mean it and find myself happy that my best friends showed up to end the silence between us. Now if only we could get our relationship back on track but I know that is easier said than done.

* * *

A howl erupts from the darkness causing my heart rate to increase as beads of sweat take up residence on my forehead. I know he's out there, hiding in the shadows. I feel him, the unknown entity who's been haunting my every sleeping moment these last few months.

I close my eyes, taking in a deep breath I remind myself this isn't real. It's only a dream.

"Dreams can be a dangerous thing for someone like you and me." His voice caused a chill to run down the length of my spine.

"Who are you?" I yell into the night as I look around, trying to keep my panic in check.

A dream can only last so long and then I'll wake up back in the safety of my bed. I can't let him, or this dream frazzle me.

"No one of importance."

"You're lying."

His tone is angry as he shouts, "Boy, do not presume to call me a liar."

"Was it not you who told me your people would find me? If you have followers or people doing your bidding, then you can't be a nobody."

He's silent for a moment before chuckling darkly.

"You are smarter than I gave you credit for."

I stand up straight. "So, who are you?"

"That is not a question you need to be asking."

"Well, I am, and I think since you're invading my dreams, you owe me an answer."

"There are more important questions you should be asking."

I sigh, "All right, I'll bite. Like what?"

"That's for you to figure out. I'm not here to give you answers or spill information. You want answers? Then ask the right questions."

I rub my eyes in frustration. "Fine," placing my hand at my side once more, I continue, "then for now, who are you? What is your name?"

He's quiet for a long while, so long I almost break the silence with another question that comes to mind.

His words send a chill through me, "I went by many names."

In a firm tone I rely, "So, give me one."

This time, his voice comes from behind me, but I don't move. "They called me Morpheus."

"That sounds like an old name," I mumbled before thinking.

"Indeed, it is." He replies with a darkness in his tone.

"You have a last name?"

He's quiet.

"Your followers, you said they are closing in on me, that they are looking for me. Why?"

His laugh echoes through the shadows around me, sending my eyes searching the pitch blackness.

"As I said, I need you."

"Yes, I remember something about being your meat suit. What does that mean?"

His tone takes on a dangerous nature as he answers, "Now, you're asking the right questions."

My heart pounds loudly in my chest. His tone reminds me of a horror movie that, even to this day, creeps me out. Freddy Krueger was always a favorite of my brother's, but his voice alone was enough to send me screaming from the room to my mother's arms. Morpheus's voice reminds me of the one villain I still can't stomach to this day.

"Well, answer me!" I yell in frustration.

"I will not show all my cards tonight, young walker."

"Why do you call me that?"

He couldn't possibly know my last name. Could he? He knew my first and this is my dream so I guess anything is possible. But again it is only a dream, nothing here is real and none of this will affect my life once I wake back up. I won't let it. These nightmares need to become a thing of the past. I can't let them take over my life, not anymore. It's time to move forward, to heal and leave the past where it belongs. In the past.

My palms turn sweaty as I hear a branch break to my left. I turn slowly as a silhouette moves in my direction.

"You do not know what you are, do you? Your family has hidden many secrets from you, boy, and by doing so, left you vulnerable and ripe for the picking. I may not be able to hold you here now or take what I want, but soon I will be able to take everything I've waited so long for, and there will be no one to stop me."

He moves closer as a patch of light runs across the left side of his face to reveal deep black pits for eyes and even darker hair to match.

"We're coming for you." He whispers.

BEEP. BEEP. BEEP.

* * *

My body shoots up into a sitting position. My lungs fight for air as my heart pounds inside my heaving chest. I'm drenched in sweat. My dream moves to the forefront of my memory, causing me to glance around my room, still feeling like I'm being watched.

It was only a dream.

I run my hands over my face, wiping the sleep from my eyes.

"So much for a nightmare-free night," I mumble.

I reach over and slam my hand down on the snooze button of my alarm clock, silencing the annoying noise, but secretly thankful for it pulling me from my latest nightmare. I notice the time reads 11:31 p.m.

Interesting.

I don't remember setting the alarm for this hour.

I discard my blanket to the foot of my bed before throwing my legs over the side. My feet touch the cool floor, waking my body instantly. Being six foot, there is nothing I can sit on where my feet don't touch the floor. I slip on my navy blue slippers and head for my bedroom door.

A snack couldn't hurt.

Once in the kitchen I open the fridge and stare at the contents inside, unsure of what to devour in my hour of need. I'm in a daze, frozen, eyes glued on the banana nut bread my mother made last night.

What did he mean?

The last thing Morpheus said to me about my family invades my mind. My mother has never lied to me, not about something important. I'm seventeen now, old enough to know about any family secrets and the skeletons in our closet. She wouldn't lie to me.

Would she?

I must be losing my mind; I'm believing something from a dream. Although, it wouldn't be the first time I heard or saw something in a dream that later came true. Maybe I'm not so crazy. I have felt something deeper going on in my family and life the last few years, and the feeling has only grown. What if my feelings and thoughts are simply, once again, making themselves known in my dreams? Is there something my parents have been hiding from me? Well, there's only one way to find out.

"Will, what are you doing up at this hour?"

My mother's voice startles me, causing me to jump as my heart rate increases once more before I release a shaky breath, turning to look at her.

"Mom."

"I'm sorry. I didn't mean to startle you." She says before closing the distance between us and placing her hand on my arm in a calming manner.

My mother has always had a touch that could soothe even the worst thoughts or fears. I never understood if it was every mother's gift or just mine. I never cared to know the answer. I knew everything would always be alright as long as I had her.

"Mom."

Worry spreads through her features. "Yes?"

No time like the present.

"Is there something… something you haven't told me? About our family, I mean."

Confusion and fear replace the worry. "What do you mean?"

Is it just me, or did that question put her on high alert?

No, you're overthinking it.

"I had this dream." I shake my head, removing the suspicion before smiling at her. "Never mind, it's nothing."

She places her hand on my cheek, "Are you sure? What was this dream about?"

I place my cool hand on her warm one and give it a light squeeze before removing it from my face, "It was nothing. Just another nightmare."

I turn to exit the kitchen, but my mother's grip on my hand stops me as her hold turns firm. "Will, you know everything I have done and continue to do is to protect you, right?"

I feel my eyebrow meet my hairline as confusion fills my mind. "Of course."

She smiles softly at me, "There is nothing I wouldn't do for you."

"I know that, Mom."

She nods her head lightly, "Good, I just needed you to know that."

I kiss her hand softly before releasing it. "And I would do anything for you."

Her smile widens as I turn away once more with a pit of fire forming in my gut, and I'm unsure if it's because I didn't grab food or if it's reacting to the weirdness of my nightmare and my mother's reaction to my question.

As I make my way back to my room, I think about two things: One, I'm glad I didn't eat anything, as I hate going to sleep with something in my stomach. Two, there might be some truth to my dreams, and my mother could be hiding something from me, and that thought alone is enough to keep me up all night.

Chapter 3

The uneasiness of first waking up engulfs me. I open my eyes, ready to take in the fuzzy view, but instead, I'm met with pitch black. I try to lift my right arm causing pins and needles to spread its length until it reaches my shoulder. My upper limb, feeling heavy, falls back down to its previous resting spot.

Arm forgotten, as I try to recall when and where I fell asleep this time, but my mind is drawing a blank. I stand and take a step forward, only to nearly fall over a hard, cold object. I feel around in the dark as my hands rest on an object, just like the one that almost had me on my ass a moment ago. The objects are on both sides of me about two feet from each other. They are as high as my waist and the tops are cold, hard and shaped like a big square. I take another step forward while leaving one hand on the object to my left and the other on my right, feeling them for a path, and then suddenly they end. Placing my hands out in front of me, I feel around the air until my hands hit a hard cool surface.

A wall.

I move my hands along it until they come to rest on a door. I feel lower until my hand rests on the knob. I try to turn it, but it won't budge, causing panic to form in my chest.

How did I get locked in this room, and where the hell am I?

I turn and make my way to the other side of the room, hoping that there will be a window I can climb through. I hit something big and solid and go flying, pain shooting up my side. Eyes finally adjusting to the darkness, I stare at the object in question as my mind tries to make sense of what my eyes are seeing.

It's a desk, which means I'm in school.

I didn't fall asleep at school, did I? If I did, someone would have woken me up. So the question remains, how did I get locked in this classroom, and how am I going to get out?

I search the far wall until I find a window. I try to open it, and despite it being unlocked, it does not move. I grab a chair from behind me and toss it at the window, waiting for the loud bang to ring through the room, but on impact, nothing happens. I watch as the chair falls to the ground in silence.

How is that possible?

The window is unscathed. I sigh in frustration as I pound my fist on the glass, immediately regretting it as a sharp pain runs up my arm.

I've never been big with small spaces and even though this is a decent sized room the thought of being trapped inside any building or room has always caused my heart to pound loudly in my chest as my body fights for air. My shrink, back when I was in grade school, called these episodes moments of anxiety that lead to panic attacks. She told me I have a fear of being locked in a space with no way out. Way to state the obvious doc.

Glancing outside, I notice an unfamiliar building across the street just as four men emerge from behind. I can tell they are searching for something or someone even from this distance but I don't recognize any of them.

The man with long bright blonde hair looks in my direction and points, "There he is, in the school."

The rest of the men peer in my direction before running towards the school. It takes me precisely five seconds for my brain to kick in and register that these men aren't here to help, but for another purpose. My mind drifts to my dreams and how Morpheus told me his men were closing in.

Don't be crazy.

Shaking my head violently, I turn away from the window, searching for another way out. Taking in a deep breath, I charge at the door on the other side of the room, my shoulder connecting with the wood forcefully. The door bursts open and sends me to the ground on the other side. I jump to my feet and head down the hallway, barely able to see a thing, as the light difference in the hall is much brighter than in the room I was just in. I run into the wall a few times before I find a door. Opening it wide, I find a small janitor's closet. I step inside and take a seat on the floor. I sit alone in the dark and wait.

Wait for them to find me.

Four against one, I don't like my odds.

What am I going to do? I can't take on four men, that much I do know. Loud footsteps echo in the hall. I close my eyes, hoping an idea will pop into my head.

"We're going to find you, little walker." One of the men says from not far down the hallway.

I hear other doors being opened and closed as I try to focus on getting out of here without being seen. My body begins to feel heavy as the room spins around me. The door opens as the earth starts shaking beneath me, but when I open my eyes, I'm no longer in a dark closet. Pine trees and bright light consume my vision. There's a twelve-foot-high dirt hill in front of me. Wanting to put as much distance between me and my pursuers as possible, I throw one foot in front of the other until I make it to the bottom of the hill. I punch my fist into the gritty dirt, testing out its density and looking for weak points. It takes me a few tries before I find a spot to start ascending the mountain of dirt. A few minutes later, I reach the top, letting my eyes scan over the landscape in front of me. There's nothing, nothing but more hills and trees.

"Will!"

I almost lose my balance as I turn around to see who is calling for me. It's a man whose voice is familiar, but not because I know the person.

"Will, we know you're here."

A new voice rings through the trees. "Come out, come out wherever you are."

They found me.

Laughter erupts among the group, and I know it's time to move my ass and fast. I move as quickly as the substance beneath my body allows, trying to spread my weight evenly. I get my one leg over the side before I hear their voices once more.

"We just want to talk to you."

"No, we just want to play with you for a little while, get inside your head and see what makes you tick."

"Come out and play, little walker."

How do they know my last name? Or is there another reason they keep saying that word? It's the same thing Morpheus kept calling me.

I try to steady myself and think of a way to get down the other side of the hill without causing bodily harm. Peering down, I don't believe that will be possible. I turn my attention in the direction where their voices were coming from, but I don't see anyone, so I plant both my hands on the top of the mound and slowly pull my left leg up and over to join my other. I almost lose my balance, but I correct it at the right moment.

"Hey, boy!"

Startled, I look up too quickly and begin to descend the other side of the dirt hill at a neck breaking pace, but not before I catch a glimpse of a group of four men hidden among the trees.

The dirt makes its way under my sleeves and the hem of my shirt, causing my skin to burn. I stifle a yelp as I continue to descend, my face burrowing further into the dirt. It's in my socks and shoes; it's covering every inch of me. Moments later, my feet hit the ground hard, causing me to lose my balance and fall backward, landing me on my back. Searing pain spreads through my right ankle and up my back, but I push the agony away and jump into a standing position. Glancing around at my surroundings, I run for the closest group of trees, hoping to disappear inside them before the men reemerge.

"Running is pointless. Whether it be now or later, we will find you. It's only a matter of time."

The man's voice becomes muffled as I move deeper into the greenage of the woods. My vision begins to blur, and my body turns heavy.

DING-DING.

"Will? Will, get up."

I open my eyes to pitch black, my arms freezing. I jolt upright to find myself sitting at my desk at school. I glance up to see Thea looking down at me, smiling as she tries to stifle a laugh. Not that I'm unhappy to see her, but what the hell is going on? I don't remember waking up or coming to school, for that matter.

Was I just asleep?

I can't remember sleeping or dreaming.

"Will?"

I look up at Thea to see she is waiting for me to follow her out the door to the next class.

"Oh, right. Sorry, I'm coming. Just give me a sec."

I reach over to grab my book bag on the floor to find it lying on my ankle. When I lift it, pins and needles begin to spread further up my leg.

"We're going to be late." I turn to see Thea still waiting at the threshold of our math class.

I hurry to get all of my books off the desk and into my black book bag.

"Coming."

As I take a step, I almost end up on the floor. I hear a giggle escape Thea as her hand meets her mouth and she turns away from me with a smile on her face.

"What's so funny?" I smile as I call after her.

"Nothing, I'm sorry."

I shake and stomp my leg on the ground to get the pins and needles feeling to subside, then I throw my book bag over my shoulder and follow Thea out the door and down the hall. Lost in thought, I place my hands in my pockets and feel something dry and grainy. I take a fistful of the substance and carefully remove my hand from my pocket. I look down as I open my hand, amazed at what I'm looking at.

Sand.

What the hell is going on?

"Will, are you OK?" Thea asks from my side.

I place my hand back in my pocket, determined to get to the bottom of what's happening, and soon.

"Yeah, I'm just not sleeping that great."

"Still having nightmares?"

I sigh. "Seems that way."

"They've gotten worse since it happened, haven't they?"

Her question makes my body halt right in the middle of the hallway.

"I'm sorry, I didn't mean..." Thea sighs.

I can see how hard it is for her and how much she wants to help but doesn't know what to say or do, and I can't say I blame her. Everything has changed, is different, and there's no going back. I'm only beginning to learn how to live in this new life without my brother and father. If I didn't have my mother, I don't know what I would do.

I don't care if she's hiding something from me. I trust my mother, and like she said last night, if she's not telling me something, it's to protect me. From what, I don't know, but I trust her to make the right decisions as she always has.

However, that doesn't change the fact that I need to get to the bottom of my dreams, and I need to know if Morpheus is dangerous. I've heard in some cases, a dream can even be fatal to the one having it, and the last thing I want is to leave my mother here alone. So, it's research time.

"Will."

I glance down at Thea, realizing I've been so deep in my thoughts, I didn't hear her talking. "I'm sorry, Thea. I'm a bit out of it today."

She giggles. "I can see that. If there is anything I can do to help, please let me know. I'm still here for you, Will."

I smile at her. "I know. Thank you. I just have a lot of things to work through."

She reaches out and takes my hand in hers before ushering us forward once more. "Well, you'll have to do that while we are sitting in our next class."

I chuckle. "Right, history."

The rest of the school day flies by, and things with Trey and Thea are great. It's like we never stopped talking to each other. It's still hard to be around them because I know it's only a matter of time before they bring up my brother and father and everything that took place last summer, and that's something I'm just not ready to talk about.

People tell you to move on and get over it, or it will be OK, but they have no idea what it feels like to not only lose your older brother but your father, too, all in the same year. People act like they know what's best and try to give advice, but at the end of the day, no one can ever know how someone else feels unless they go through the same thing. All I want is to return to a normal life, whatever that is. I don't want to be known as the guy who lost it all last year and has gone a bit off his rocker, yup that's what some people are saying. More than anything that's what I not only want but need, well that and to get to the bottom of these dreams so I can finally put them behind me.

"Looks like a lot of homework for us tonight, huh, Will?"

Thea's voice pulls me out of my head as I turn to look at her, only to wish I hadn't. Sometimes I forget that she can read me like an open book.

"Will, what is it?"

I look away from her before I answer, "I'm fine."

"No, you're not. You seem to forget how well I know you. You don't have to act like you're fine, not around me." Before she finishes her sentence, her hand is wrapped around my arm, and she turns me around to face her. She pauses to look at me, but only for a moment. "I know this can't be easy for you, and I won't pretend to know what you're going through, but you need to talk to someone, you need to let it out, and you need to do it soon. I can see it in your eyes. It's consuming you."

I place my free hand on hers and gently remove her hand from my arm, the look on her face cuts me deep. "You're right. But, I'm just not ready yet."

Thea closes her eyes, releasing a sigh. "I understand. Just know I'm here for you. I'm not going anywhere, and please think about talking with someone, and soon. It's not good to hold things in, especially things this heavy."

I can't help but smile at her as I reply, "OK."

We both turn around, not taking our eyes off of each other when, bam!

My shoulder hits something hard, followed by loud thuds. I peel my eyes away from Thea to take in a girl with shoulder-length fawn hair. She's on the ground picking up her books. It's the new girl. I noticed her back in September, but no one really bothers with her. Not sure if it's because of the kill stare she gives to everyone who gets too close, or if it's for another reason entirely.

I bend down and reach for the closest book. "I'm so sorry. I wasn't watching where I was going."

"I can see that," she replies as she takes the book out of my hands, never looking in my direction.

"I hope I didn't hurt you."

"Hurt me?" She laughs. "Hurt my books, maybe, and maybe making your girlfriend a little jealous, but I'm fine."

I look up to find Thea looking down at us.

Laughing, I turn my focus back to the girl collecting her last book off the ground and returning it to the rest in her hands. "She's not my girlfriend."

She looks at me for the first time, her gaze taking my breath away.

She's beautiful and not in the obvious over-the-top kind of way. Her eyes are breathtaking charcoal, and her skin is untouched. Her lips have the perfect curve to them but her small dimples are what my eyes come to focus on. She notices me staring a moment later, forcing me to look away as I move back into a standing position. I look down at her as I offer my hand, causing her to roll her eyes before taking it reluctantly.

"Thank you," she says as she turns away from me and heads down the hall.

For a moment, I pause, unsure of what to do, but then I turn to Thea, telling her I'll be right back before I run down the hall after the nameless girl.

"Hey, wait up."

She stops but doesn't turn to face me. Instead, I move around to stand in front of her. Annoyance is written all over her face, but I don't let it phase me.

"My name's Will. You're the new girl."

"Wow, you are a bright lad, give him an A-plus."

Ignoring her jab, I continue, "Having a bad first day back at school, I take it?"

"Right again, you should be given an award for observation skills."

A smile creeps on my face, "Listen, I'm sorry about what happened back there. I'm not normally that clumsy."

"As I told you before, it's all good."

"Obviously not from all the hostility you're throwing my way."

For the first time, a smirk appears on her face as she turns away, obviously not wanting me to notice, which only makes my smile grow. I don't know what it is about her, but I'm drawn to her. It's like I have no control over my body or words that come from my mouth. I've never really cared much about other girls, not to the point of being the one to give chase, at least. But something is different about her. I can't put my finger on it, but I know I want to get to know her. I've only felt this way about one other girl in my life and she's been my best friend since.

"Let me get you lunch tomorrow, my way of making it up to you."

She turns her focus back to me, her smile gone. "It's cool. There's no need for that."

"I know, but I want to."

"You're not going to let this go, are you?"

I shake my head as she releases a sigh.

"Fine. Lunch. Tomorrow."

"Wait, I never got your name." I say to her as she gets ready to walk away.

"You're a smart lad, I'm sure you can learn it on your own." She walks past me and out the front doors.

Chapter 4

"How was the first day of the second half of your senior year?" My mother's voice takes on an excited tone.

I shrug, "Same as Junior, Sophomore, and Freshman year. Nothing new."

My run-in with the new girl pops into my mind as the corner of my mouth creeps up on my face.

My mother slaps me lightly on the shoulder. When I look up, her know-it-all smile is staring back. "Who is she?"

Taken aback, my eyes widen. "Who's who?"

She sighs. "The girl you met."

"How did you know I met a girl?"

She crosses her arms over her chest, proudly looking at me. "Mothers know everything."

I chuckle. "Apparently."

"Well, what's her name?"

I sigh as I turn away from her and head for the kitchen, suddenly needing a cold drink. "Sage."

After our run in I went back to Thea and asked her if she knew the new girl's name. Of course she gave me hell saying how I should have known it since we have a lot of the same classes together. Normally she would be right but since I've been in my own little world till just recently anything around me kind of went unnoticed. So, when they introduced her to all the new classes back in September I kind of closed off and didn't register her

32

name. Thea, realizing where my head was, apologized and told me her name was Sage.

My mother's tone changes to one I don't recognize. "That's an interesting name."

"Interesting name for an interesting girl," I mumble.

"What's that mean?"

I open the fridge and pull out the orange juice, pulp-free, just the way I like it. I pull off the cap bringing the jug to my lips.

"Will Walker," my mother says in her serious tone before pulling the jug away from my lips right before they touch. "How many times do I need to tell you?"

We say in unison, "No drinking out of the cartons."

I look at her playfully as she grunts in annoyance.

"Get a glass, please."

I turn away, reach inside the cabinet, pull out a plastic cup and pour the cool contents inside before returning the container to the fridge. I retrieve my cup, gesturing to my mother with it.

"Is that better?"

She nods with a smile. "Much."

"Good."

"You know it's important to learn and live by these things. What woman is going to want to date, let alone marry, a man who drinks straight from the carton?"

I choke on the juice at her words. "I don't know, Mom. Definitely not a seventeen-year-old girl."

"Woman."

My eyebrow rises. "Huh."

"Note of advice: no female likes to be called a girl. We prefer woman, just like men don't like to be called boys."

I shake my head with a slight smile on my face. "Fine, woman."

She nods. "That's better. Now, back to the topic at hand."

"Which one?" I laugh.

"The girl you met today, tell me about her."

"You mean woman." I smile.

"Correct."

I place my now empty cup in the sink adding water. "She's interesting."

"Meaning?"

"I don't know. There's something about her that I can't explain."

When I look at my mother, I notice worry hidden just under the surface of her smile, and for the second time since my nightmare, I wonder if she really could be hiding something from me and if so what could it be?

"Well, get your homework and studies done and get some rest. I'm headed into work." She kisses me on the cheek. "I'll see you tomorrow, honey."

Making her way to the front door, she grabs her winter jacket off the rack. Fall is right around the corner, and with my mother's petite figure the New Jersey air makes her cold quickly. Williamstown can be known as one of the nicer Jersey towns, but everywhere feels the same for me. It is nice to have a lake right across the street, though. That's where we live, back in the Lakes of Williamstown, but if I had it my way, I would love to move to Florida right by the ocean.

"Have a good day at work, Mom."

"Thank you, honey, don't forget."

I cut her off as I roll my eyes. "Yes, homework, dinner, and a good night's rest."

"You got it."

"Love you, Mom."

She opens the door. "Love you, too."

As the door closes behind her for the first time, I find myself hoping for one of my nightmares tonight. Maybe then, I'll get some answers.

Chapter 5

The one time I want my heart rate racing is the one time I have a peaceful night's sleep. So much for answers. The first half of the school day flew by. Now, it's lunchtime. I can't remember the last time I was this nervous about being around a girl.

I enter the cafeteria, eyes scanning the crowd. I find her a moment later sitting alone at an empty table. A smile creeps on my face as I head over.

"Can I join you?"

She glances up at me in a daze. "Well, you did make me agree to lunch, so, I guess so."

I place my bag on the table and pull my lunch out. "How was the rest of your day yesterday?"

"I didn't get run over by any more classmates, so I guess that's one for the win column."

I sigh, placing my turkey sandwich on the napkin in front of me. "I'm sorry, again. Normally I'm more aware of my surroundings."

"So you've mentioned."

I rub the back of my neck nervously.

"What is there to do around here for fun anyway?"

I chuckle. "Not much, honestly."

She turns her attention back to her book. "Bummer."

"What are you reading?"

She lifts the book high enough to give me a view of the title, *Wake by Lisa McMann.*

"What's it about?"

Her eyes filled with annoyance as she mumbles, "A girl who gets pulled into people's dreams, even if she doesn't want to."

"Interesting."

"Very."

I take a bite of my sandwich, unsure of what to say next, becoming very aware that even though she agreed to this lunch, she would rather be alone. So many things have changed in my life this past year, and I find it hard to catch my breath most of the time. Now there's another cherry on top of all the bullshit that has become my life. This girl—*sorry, woman*—I can't put my finger on why I want to be around her as much as I do; I've never really cared much about the opposite sex. If I'm being honest, Thea was the only girl I ever really noticed, but she's one of my best friends, and that's a line you never cross.

I feel stuck in a dream, like this book Sage is reading. I've been sucked into someone else's life, someone else's nightmare, and it only gets worse the deeper I go. My brother's mysterious death, my father's abrupt departure, and these dark dreams feel like they are only the beginning.

As much as I know that Morpheus is simply a figment of my imagination made from the rift in my life, I can't help but find some truth in what he said. My mother has been acting weird about certain things that she never did before, and I can't help but wonder why. Then, there's Sage. I know new students come and go all the time, but for some reason, the timing for me and the vibe I get from her tells me there's more to it.

Will, get a grip.

I close my eyes, swallowing my food. *I'm losing my mind.*

"Is it true your brother died and your father left?"

My mouth goes dry as my heart stops in my chest. *Did she really just ask me that?*

"I'm sorry. I've been told I don't have a filter."

"I..."

Her eyes widen. "So, it is true."

"Um."

36

She looks excited as she places her book down on the table and leans in closer to me. "Is your last name Walker?"

My ears start ringing, and I can't think. I nod.

She leans back, "Wow. Interesting."

I'm at a loss for words. Did she just call me interesting? Or is she only interested in my now topsy-turvy life?

Before I can ask, she's packing up her bag and standing. "I'll catch you later, Walker."

The emphasis in which she says my name sends a chill down my spine as she turns and walks away from the table, giving me the perfect view of her ass in her pitch-black leggings. My heart drops in my stomach as my eyes refuse to look away.

Stop it!

What is wrong with me?

Chapter 6

What is it about this girl that gets under my skin so much, and why is she so interested in me all of a sudden? She couldn't stand me until she knew I was a Walker, and my family was ripped apart. Since our lunch three weeks ago, she has acknowledged me whenever we see one another, and she even starts our conversations. Since that day, we have had lunch together at least two times a week. I don't know if I would call it lunch, more like an interrogation. At least that's the way it felt sometimes. She would ask me about my life and how I felt since my world imploded. She even asked me about my dreams and how I've been sleeping since it happened. It almost felt like she knew something she wasn't sharing. She shrugged it off, saying how she took psychology or something at her last school and learned how when we are asleep, our subconscious can make our dreams dark by making them about something we are trying to suppress.

"So, the new girl," Thea's words pull me from my thoughts.

"What about her?"

"What is it with you and playing dumb lately? Especially when we both know you're anything but."

I sigh. "I'm not playing dumb. I just don't understand your statement."

"Are you really going to make me say the words?"

I turn to look at her, but we both keep walking. "I guess I am."

She sighs. "Fine. How was lunch today?"

I face forward again. "It was different."

"Different in a good way?"

"I don't know, just different."

She stops walking, and I do the same. I turn around to look at her before she says. "Will, you seem like the old you again."

"Is something wrong with that?"

She takes a step towards me and then takes my hand in hers. As she looks down at them, she says, "I'm glad we are talking again." She looks up at me. "And more than that, I'm happy you're coming out of your shell and starting to feel normal again, but," she pauses and looks back at our hands, "I'm worried about you."

"There's nothing to worry about."

"You can keep saying that, but I know you well enough to know that's not the truth. You're different now." She squeezes my hand. "I feel it. A part of you is missing."

"My brother's dead, Thea. What did you expect?"

She looks at me sadly. "I didn't mean it like that. I expected his death to change you. Losing a brother would change anyone."

"Then what's the problem?"

"The problem is something is off. I can feel it. You're darker, somehow."

"Darker?"

"Maybe I'm using the wrong words. I don't know how to explain it, but I know something is going on with you. Something is scaring you."

I try to make light of the conversation as I release a chuckle. "Me? Scared? Come on."

She looks at me with knowing eyes. "Will."

I sigh. "All right. All right."

I turn and start walking again. She doesn't let go of my hand, but starts walking by my side again.

I look down and smile at her. "Having you back in my life is making more of a difference than you realize."

She stops us again and hugs me. "I've missed you."

"I've missed you too."

She releases me, and we continue walking. My mind runs away, reliving last month's nightmares when I met Morpheus. I can't get him out of my mind since the last dream I had.

"So, what are your plans for the weekend?"

"Nothing really planned."

I notice a smile creep up on her face before she says, "Well, maybe we can do something. It's been a long time. I would like to catch up on what's new with you."

"Nothing new. Same old Will, just a different day. But sure, I would like to get together. Just let me know what works for you."

"Tomorrow."

I smile. "OK. Tomorrow, it is."

"I know Trey would like you to come over."

I look at her, surprised. "Why do you say that?"

"Because he still feels bad about everything and he kind of felt like you've been avoiding him since we returned to school."

"I haven't."

"I know, but he doesn't think that."

I take a deep breath. "I'll talk to him about it."

"Just don't tell him I said anything."

I laugh. "I won't."

"Good." She smiles as she looks forward again. "I just hope you two can get back the friendship you had before."

"I think that's going to take some time."

"Understandable."

We walk in silence for a while until her house comes into view.

"Will?"

I turn to look back at her. "Yeah?"

"I'm sorry."

"For what?" I ask, confused.

"For not being there like I should have been, like I wanted to be."

I close my eyes and take in a slow breath before answering her. "Thea, you don't need to apologize. I understand."

"It's no excuse. We were your friends—best friends—, and we should have been there for you. Whether we were uncomfortable or not, you needed us, and at that moment, we weren't there for you." She looks down and away from me. "I wasn't there."

I reach over and place my hand on hers. "Thea, please don't beat yourself up over this. You are here now when it matters most. When it first happened, and even just last month, I was too shut off, too angry, to even try to deal or talk about it, let alone allow anyone to be there for me. It wouldn't have mattered, trust me."

She still doesn't look at me, so I move my hand under her chin and turn her face towards me. "I'm not mad, so please don't beat yourself up over this anymore."

I give her a look, and she knows what I'm waiting for. She locks eyes with me and nods her head. I smile and start leading us up to her walkway.

As we reach her front door, she smiles at me. "I'll see you tomorrow."

"See you tomorrow."

I didn't go straight home after walking Thea home as I planned. Instead, I walked with no destination in mind. I just kept going. When my feet finally started to hurt, I saw the sky was getting dark, and I knew my mother would be home soon, so I stopped at a nearby minimart and grabbed us something to have for dinner, then I headed home.

I take the last step to our front door and release a breath. I try to think back to when life was easier. Not too long ago, I would walk up the sidewalk and be able to hear mom, dad, and West laughing from inside the house. But now, it's always so dark and quiet that the pit in my stomach always grows to twice its size when I come home.

I walk in the front door, thinking I would find my mother in the kitchen, but everything's dark. I know she's home because I saw her car in the driveway. *Maybe she went to bed early.*

I place dinner on the counter and head to my room to change, and that's when I hear her. She's in her room, but she's not asleep. She's crying. I close my eyes, hating that there's nothing I can do for her. I can't even make myself feel better, so how am I supposed to help her? I feel the anger burning in my gut, and in my mind, I slowly count back from a hundred, trying to ground myself again, but instead, I go somewhere else entirely.

* * *

"Will, come on. Let's go to the lake. It should be frozen by now." West's voice travels from the kitchen to me sitting on the couch.

I jump up, all excited. "Heck yeah."

He starts to put on his coat and gloves but stops to look at me. "What's wrong?"

"Shouldn't we wake mom and let her know where we are going?"

He stops what he's doing, walks over to the end table, opens the drawer, and pulls out a pen and paper. "No, she's tired. She had a long shift. We can leave a note for her in case she wakes up before we get back."

I smile as I feel the excitement bubbling to the surface. "What should I bring?"

"Bring the football for us to toss around." I head to the closet and retrieve the said object as West calls to me, "Make sure you dress warmly."

I grab the football and head to my room to double up my socks and throw a hoodie over my head. When I return to the living room, West is ready and waiting for me with my jacket in his hands.

"Here, I'll help you put it on," he says while holding it up.

I turn my back to him and slide one arm through a sleeve, then the other. When I'm done, I turn around to face West, and he takes the football from me so I can zip up my jacket. I place my gloves on my hands then look up at him.

"All set."

"OK. Let's go," he says with excitement as he passes me the football.

The lake was only a few blocks away, so we got there in no time. West runs out to the lake edge and turns around to face me with his hands up.

"Throw it here."

I smile and toss the football in his direction.

He catches it and yells, "Touch down!"

I start laughing.

He goes to the water's edge and puts a foot down on the ice. I run over to his side frantically. "Be careful, West!"

"Don't worry, little brother," he says with a smile.

He moves his foot all around, feeling the ice and applying some pressure as he goes. He turns to me and smiles before putting his other foot on the frozen lake, and it takes everything in me to stop myself from grabbing for him.

He smiles. "See, little brother? I told you it was all frozen. Come on, let's skate around for a bit."

I shake my head.

"Come on, don't be a chicken."

"I'm not."

"Will's being a little chicken."

"Stop it."

He looks at me and smiles. "Come on, little brother. You really think I would let anything happen to you?"

I look at him, knowing his words are true, but something in me is screaming to walk away. "I know you wouldn't."

He reaches out his hand to me. "Then trust me. Come on."

West has always been the dangerous one out of both of us, always taking chances when he shouldn't. I would always follow in his footsteps, not because he was my bigger brother, and not because he asked me to, but because I felt this need. Something always made me follow him, but this time, something felt wrong.

"West, I think we should be getting back."

His smile fades. "We just got here."

"But, if mom wakes up, she's going to be mad we left."

"We are only a few blocks from home. What's the point of me finally turning thirteen if I can't take us out?"

I look down at my feet.

I want to move them.

I want to join my brother on the icy playground.

But something keeps pulling me back.

Something keeps telling me it isn't safe.

"Please, West."

He must have seen how scared I was because his face changed to one not of annoyance, but understanding.

"OK, little brother. I'm coming." He started to walk back to the edge slowly as he

lifted his arm and yelled, "Will, catch."

As he releases the ball, the hole in my stomach deepens as I watch my brother fall through the ice.

* * *

My mother's sobs pull me back as I shake my head. I creep to my bedroom, not wanting to disturb her. I figure the best thing to do is go to bed early and try to let go of all the sadness that we still have wrapped up inside.

That day, I was so afraid my brother would die, but thankfully, someone nearby saw and sprung into action and saved him. Best believe West listened to me a little more after that day, especially after we got home and our father chewed into him in a colossal way. Our mother was livid, but knowing we were safe tempered her anger. Our father made us promise never to do something so reckless again, and we didn't, at least not for another five years.

My brother was eighteen, and I was seventeen when he felt it was time to live on the wild side again, at least for a night. I remember him saying, clear as day, *"What could go wrong?"*

Little did we know everything was about to go wrong. Because we were older, stronger, and more intelligent, we thought that nothing could happen like it did on that day five years before.

Boy, were we wrong.

* * *

I've been here before. It feels memorable, but I can't make out the picture around me yet.

"Will."

I spin in the direction that I heard someone whisper my name. The voice sounds so familiar. It sounds like...but it can't be.

West?

Frantically, I look all around me, but there's no one in sight.

"Will." The voice travels to me again but sounds further away now.

44

I start to run in the direction I think it's coming from.

"Will, you need to know what's coming. I need you to find me." The voice is even lower now, almost impossible to hear.

"West!" I shout.

I can feel him, but I feel like I'm losing him all over again. I run as fast as my legs can carry me until I trip over something on the ground, and my face gets covered in a cloud of dirt. I fight back a choke and straighten myself up once more and run like I've never run before.

"Find me, Will."

Panic starts to set in.

Another voice comes to me from the darkness.

"Will. Wake up! Will!"

It sounds like Thea, and she sounds scared.

I can feel myself starting to be pulled in the direction of her voice. As hard as I'm fighting to stay to look for my brother, I'm losing the fight. As I'm flown into the night sky, I scream for my brother once more, just like when we were kids.

"West!"

His voice, at a whisper, calls to me before I'm too far gone.

"Will, you have to remember. Remember what happened. Then, you need to come find me. Find the truth, and then find me."

* * *

Slammed back into my body, I shoot up into a sitting position, causing my forehead to collide with something. I move away from the object and nurse my forehead before looking up to see Thea doing the same.

"Thea?"

Her eyes reveal her nervousness that she's in my bedroom. She jumps off my bed faster than I've ever seen her move.

"Sorry, I knocked, but no one answered the door, and I knew you were home since we were supposed to get together this morning. Then I heard you back here, and when I came in, it looked like you were having a horrible dream, so I wanted to wake you up."

I rub my eyes anxiously before turning to look at her. She looks beautiful. Breathtaking. Before I can avert my eyes, she scratches the back of her head and turns away from me, and I know she noticed me staring.

Nice going.

"Sorry, I'll wait in the living room. You should get dressed."

For the first time, I realize I'm wearing no shirt or pants, leaving me very exposed. Without another word, she walks out and closes the door behind her.

Chapter 7

I find Thea standing in the living room staring out the window, lost in her thoughts.

"Hey."

She turns around, exposing a smile. "Hey, yourself." Closing the distance between us, she says, "I'm sorry. I shouldn't have just let myself in like that."

"No, it's fine. I'm glad you did because I doubt I would have woken up on my own and," I pause, unsure if I should say the following words, "and I was looking forward to today. It's been a while since we've had a chance to hang out. Just the two of us."

"I know. My brother was always pushing himself into our little twosome." Giggling, she continues, "he was so determined to make it a threesome, so determined that it worked."

"Well, you know Trey. When he sets his mind to something, he always gets it."

"You can say that again. He's always been pretty intimidating."

"Speaking of your brother, where is he this morning?"

Smiling, she replies, "Still in bed."

I rub the back of my neck sheepishly. "Oh."

Her smile widens. "Seems men sleep in late."

Our eyes lock as we erupt into laughter.

"But I told him we would come over later and pick him up. I know he was looking forward to getting together today."

"Oh."

"As I mentioned earlier, he feels like he needs some time with you. We both feel like we let you down, and he wants to try to mend the relationship you once had."

"I already told you both—"

She raises a hand, silencing me. "I know, you understand." She drops her hand. "But like I've told you, it wasn't OK, and we don't feel good about it. We didn't do the right thing by you."

Ready to change the subject, I counter, saying, "Well, I'm looking forward to seeing him outside of school, too. The last time, I wasn't on my best behavior."

With a smile, she turns her attention to the couch. "Can we sit?"

"Oh, yeah, I'm sorry. Please, sit. Do you want anything to drink?"

She takes the seat closest to where she was standing and sighs. "Will, are you OK? No games."

"Yeah, I'm fine. Why do you always ask me that?"

"That didn't seem like a normal dream to me and, well, you seem more off than usual since I woke you up."

I rub the back of my neck, not wanting to talk about my recent dream or even think about it, for that matter.

"You can tell me." Thea reaches over and places her hand on mine, causing all my defenses, all my walls, to crash down around me.

How can one person have so much control over you?

Like my mother, a calm washes over me whenever we are close, while at the same time, every nerve in my body is screaming.

"It's not something I'm ready to talk about."

"Is it West?"

It's been such a long time since we hung out that I keep forgetting how well she knows me. "Yeah."

My eyes travel towards the door, my body wanting to make a run for it, but then her hand closes tightly around mine, sending a warmth running through my body as tranquility washes over me. I haven't felt this grounded in over a year. Turning my gaze back to her, I can see my pain mirroring in her eyes.

"I…" my mind wants to go blank. I don't want to remember. "I was somewhere dark and alone. At least I thought I was alone. But then," I look at her, unsure if I should continue, only to find her eyes urging me forward, "then, I heard West."

I wait for her to tell me I've officially snapped, or maybe try to explain why I might be hearing my dead brother, but instead, she asks, "What do you mean, you heard West?"

The words come rushing out of my mouth like water down a waterfall before I can stop them. "He told me I had to remember and that…that I had to find him once I did."

The skin on her forehead wrinkles as her eyebrows reach her hairline. "Find him? Remember? Remember what?"

Feeling frustrated with myself, I pull my hand from hers, stand up, and begin pacing.

"I don't know. It was so confusing. I mean, I try to go back to that day, but every time I do, it's like a blank page."

The next thing I know, Thea is standing next to me, holding both my hands.

"You're blocking out that day because you don't want to remember, and I can't say I blame you. But, your subconscious is screaming at you to remember for a reason. I know it's hard, and it sucks, and I'm sure you don't want to, but I think you need to. Your mind needs you to. And if you need to do it alone, I understand." She squeezes my hands lightly, then continues, "But if you want me here, I will be. I'm here if you want me to help you sort through the cobwebs. If you need a shoulder to cry on and someone there to listen, I'm your girl. I just want you to know that. Whatever you need, I'll be here." Her hands squeeze mine again. "I won't disappear this time."

Without thinking, I lift her hand to my lips and place a light kiss on her skin. I look up at her, and our eyes lock. For the first time, I feel like I see what I've always dreamed would be there in her eyes. But before I can act on it, she speaks.

"So, you wanna talk more about it? Or you wanna watch a movie while we wait for my slacker brother to wake up?" She asks with a smile.

"Um, movie it is. We can deal with the craziness of my life and dreams another day."

She pulls back. "What movie are we going to watch?"

"Good question." I look over to the three tall shelves next to the TV to see our vast selection. "What kind of movie are you in the mood for?"

"I guess a comedy would be nice."

I turn away from her and walk over to the shelves, and whisper to myself, "Yeah, it would."

"What?"

I turn to her and smile. "Nothing."

I look over the comedy section and find one that I remember she liked and throw it in the player. I return to the couch and sit next to her once more with a massive smile on my face.

"What did you put in?" She asks with a laugh.

"You'll see."

"Will." She smiles at me as she reaches over and tries to take the remote from me, and we end up in a wrestling match for it.

Then the movie's main menu comes on the screen. "Will, I love this movie."

"I know."

"You remembered?" Her eyes shine with excitement mixed with surprise, "But we watched this, like—"

I cut her short with a smile, "Four years ago."

Looking at me in awe, she mumbles, "How did you remember?"

Bumping her shoulder with mine, I whisper playfully, "I pay attention." I raise the remote and hit play as she continues to stare at me. I laugh. "Let's watch the movie."

It takes her a minute, but then she turns her attention back to the screen just in time to see the name pop up: *The Proposal*. I remember the first time we watched it together with her brother, my parents, and my brother. By the middle of the film, we were the only two still watching it. My mother would have been too, but she was cooking dinner, and my father decided he would have more fun helping her than finishing the movie. Both of our brothers chose to go out and toss around the football instead. Sitting here with her now, I try to go back to that day, to recreate it. I close my eyes, trying to imagine the laughter of my parents coming from the kitchen as my father rubbed some of the flour on my mother's face. Once I hear it, I smile, then focus on the guys outside throwing the ball, calling each other names. Once I have it, I open my eyes and watch the movie in bliss, sitting next to my best friend.

After the movie ended, we left to pick up Trey and grab a bite to eat. As we pull up to their house, Trey runs up the walkway in our direction. I glance down at my hand, still intertwined with Thea's. I make a conscious decision and remove my hand from hers before Trey reaches the car.

"Hey, guys. I was wondering when you were going to show up."

"Sorry, we were watching a movie." I glance at Thea before teasing, "Plus, I heard you were sleeping in. Wouldn't want to mess with your beauty sleep."

"Haha," he mumbles while opening the back door.

Thea laughs. "How else will you keep up with the rest of the team?"

"Guess it's pick-on-Trey day," he says while flashing his pearly whites. "Go ahead and do your worst, but first, I need sustenance. I could eat a horse." Then looking at me, he asks, "Where are we going for a bite?"

I look at Thea as she says with a smile, "I know just the place."

* * *

We pull up to our destination as Trey says from the back seat, "Oh, man, talk about bringing back memories."

Thea smiles and whispers, "Is this OK?"

I nod. "More than OK."

The *All-Day Breakfast* sign catches my attention, causing a smile to spread across my face. Nothing is better than breakfast at any time of the day, in my opinion. My gaze travels a little higher to the *Pete's Diner* sign as we head inside.

It's been over a year since I was here. Thea, Trey, and I would come here at least once a week after school. My family and I would also come here every other weekend for dinner. I have a lot of memories in this place, more than my friends know.

We take a seat at a booth in the back since an elderly couple occupies our regular table. Once we are seated, our waitress comes over with a bright smile on her face, but her eyes hold a different story. I see the sadness hiding in them.

"What can I get you to drink?"

"Water, please," Thea says.

"And for you, sir?"

"I'll take a sweet tea and a coffee." Trey answers.

Turning her attention to me, her smile widens. "And for you...Will?"

Thea and Trey look at her in surprise before I answer.

"I'll have water, as well, please."

"Coming right up."

She walks away, leaving Thea and Trey confused as they look from her back to me a few times before Trey asks, "What was that?"

"What?" I ask.

"Dude, she knew you by name."

I shrug. "So?"

"You don't think that's a little weird? Or creepy?"

I smile. "No, I used to come here all the time."

"Yeah, we all did."

"No, I mean yeah, I came here with you, but I also came here with my family a few times a month, too. We would usually have her as our waitress."

Thea and Trey look at each other with blank expressions before Thea says, "I didn't know."

"Thea, it's fine. I love it here."

They look at each other, unsure as I bury my head in the menu to ignore them.

"So, Will," Trey says as he slaps me on the back. "What's been going on? It's been a while. I would like to catch up."

"Why are you acting weird?" I ask.

He removes his hand as his smile falters. "Just trying to catch up. It's been forever."

My eyebrow lifts, causing Trey to sigh before continuing.

"I'm sorry. I don't know the right way to go about this. I'm trying." He rubs the back of his neck nervously. "I just don't know where to go from here."

"You don't need to try so hard, Trey."

"I just want things to go back to the way they were before. I'm trying to close the gap, but I don't know how."

I look away. "I don't think that's possible."

"I know. I should never have turned my back on you. Not when you needed me most. I was a shitty friend for that. I'm trying to do better."

I look at him. "That's not what I meant."

The realization becomes clear on his face. "Oh, I—sorry."

"It's fine."

"See, as I said, I don't know what to say and what not to say around you anymore."

"Trey, it's cool."

"No, it's not. I couldn't imagine if something had happened to Thea or you. I don't know how I would react, so it's hard to figure this out. Losing your brother and your father walking out…. It's not fair, and I know things are different now, but Thea and I are here for you. We weren't before, and we should have been, but we are trying to make things right."

"Well, maybe start by not bringing it up."

"See. I don't know how to shut my mouth. I'm doing this all wrong."

"Dude, seriously, chill. It's fine. It will take us some time to figure out how to move forward and deal with all these…changes. It's going to take time before things feel normal again, or close to normal."

"I just want you to know I'm here. I know he was your brother, and no one can replace him, and I'm not trying to, but I hope you can consider me like your brother because I consider you as more than just a friend."

I smile at him. "I know, and I do, too."

He exhales with a smile. "Good."

"Want to throw around the ball for a bit when we get back?"

"Heck yeah."

* * *

The rest of our time together went off without a hitch. Trey finally settled back into his skin. It was hard to be around him before he did. I could feel his uneasiness the whole time, and it was making me feel more on edge than usual. I feel better now that we talked and got the past behind us. They know I don't hold any hard feelings about them not being around after everything happened, but I can tell they still feel horrible about it. I wish I could do something to get them to understand it doesn't matter to me. I have other things to be mad about, and having them back in my life has lessened the emptiness I've been feeling.

My brother was always there, and we did everything together. Being without him hasn't been easy, but when you take him and my father and the absence of my two best friends and mix it all together, life becomes very lonely and dark. My mother has been my saving grace these past months, and I don't know what I would do without her but now having Thea and Trey back has made that darkness a little less dark and it couldn't have come at a more needed time in my life. I'm more grateful for them then they will ever know.

Chapter 8

It's dark and quiet when I finally get home. I guess this is my new normal, being alone and left to myself more often than not. I head to the kitchen and get started on dinner. When I finish, I glance at the clock on the stove: 7:58 p.m.

That's weird. Mom should have been home by now.

After I ate my fill, I put away the leftovers and made a plate for my mom to have when she made it home. Then, I head to my room and flop myself down on my bed. Sleep takes me quickly.

* * *

My body is drifting into the darkness. Afraid to go any deeper, I try to wake up. I can't hear my brother's cries, not again. I fall deeper and deeper unwilling to open my eyes until I feel my feet settle on solid ground. I open them reluctantly and they struggle to adjust to the change from darkness to light.

I'm in my kitchen.

"Will."

The voice coming to me from the living room sounds familiar.

Confused, I relocate to the room to find Sage sitting on the couch.

"Are you going to come sit down and watch the movie with me, or what?" She asks with a grin.

I walk over and sit next to her on the couch as she reaches for the remote and turns the movie on.

"What movie did you pick?"

Her smile widens. "Guess you'll just have to wait and see."

I settle into my seat comfortably, and a moment later, I look down to find Sage's hand now on top of mine. I look at her smiling face, confused.

Why is she here?

Why is she smiling?

This girl hates my guts. Yes, we've been having civil lunches lately, but this isn't normal. Sage pulls me from my thoughts as she removes her hand from mine to brush back a strand of beautiful, dark brown hair that fell in her face.

Something isn't right. This can't be real. What is she doing in my home? We've talked a lot over the last month but never went to each other's homes. We exchanged numbers and texted on occasion, but only about homework assignments.

"Will?"

"Yeah."

She looks away shyly. "You like me, right?"

I practically choke on my next words. "Of course, I like you."

"No, Will, I mean," she pauses for a moment, seeming unsure of her following words, "I mean you like me, like me, right?"

I feel the blood rushing to my cheeks as they turn hot, and I have to look away. I don't know what to say or how to answer the question without embarrassing myself. More than that, though, I don't know how to answer it, period. I barely know the girl, yet the pull I feel towards her and the emotions that come to the surface in her presence are like how I am with Thea. But, I've known Thea my whole life, and I've loved her for years. Sage, well, I don't know her. So, why do I feel this strongly about her?

"Will?"

"I, um."

I begin to stand, but she grabs my wrist and pulls me back down to the couch. I'm not ready to look at her, but I know she needs an answer.

I mumble, "Yes."

"Yes? As in you like me, like me?"

"Yes, Sage. I like you, like you. Why are you even asking me that?"

I turn to look at her, and my lips are met with hers. At first, I'm stiff from surprise or shock, not sure which. Her kiss feels urgent, almost as if this is something she's been waiting for. Before I can stop myself, my hand moves to her waist, and I pull her closer, but she doesn't let it end there. She keeps moving until she's on top of me. I lower myself down until my back is flat on the couch.

My body is reacting on its own as my hand travels up the hem of her shirt and rests against her hot bare skin. Sage doesn't react the way I would expect her to. Instead of pushing me off of her, she presses her body against mine until every inch of us is touching.

Panting, needing to catch my breath, I separate our lips and move her chocolate-colored hair away from her neck. Before I can stop myself, my lips touch the naked area gently. Something out of the corner of my eye draws my attention, sending me to turn in that direction.

There, standing only five feet away from the couch, is Sage, and she looks almost as surprised as I do.

"Sage?"

I look from Sage standing over me, then up to the Sage on top of me and back again. I quickly lift Sage off me, surprised when she doesn't say a word.

The Sage standing a few feet away wears a shocked expression. "Will? I hoped I was wrong."

"Wrong about what? What's going on?"

"You're a dream walker."

"A what?"

She begins to look around the living room, with what almost looks like panic on her face. She moves to retreat but I jump off the couch to follow her. I grab her wrist lightly, making her turn back around to face me.

"Not here. It's not safe."

"What are you talking about?" I plead.

"Will, I promise we will talk, but not here."

I look back at the couch seeing the other Sage still sitting there unmoving.

"This is a dream, isn't it?" I ask.

"Yes."

"But how? How are you here? How is this even possible?"

Fear is evident in her eyes as she glances frantically around the room. "Please.

Wake yourself up, and we can talk. I promise I'll tell you everything I know, but not here, not now."

I look down at her wrist before releasing her, but she moves away from me, then starts to fade into the darkness.

"Wake up, Will."

Her voice is the last thing I hear before I start to fall.

* * *

I wake up on the couch and slowly bring my hands to my eyes, rubbing at them feverishly. A dream. It was only a dream. The clock reads 11:48 p.m, only mere minutes away from Sunday morning. Before I get off the couch, I notice a blanket on my lap, and I instantly realized my mom must have come home and found me asleep here and instead of waking me, she covered me with a blanket. A new thought crosses my mind.

How did I get on the couch?

I remember coming home, making dinner, and walking to my room. I remember flopping on the bed and sleep taking me over, even though it was still early in the day.

Did I sleepwalk?

I slowly pry myself off the couch and make my way to my mother's room to find her sound asleep in her bed, glad my dream didn't wake her up like they usually do lately. I turn away and head to my room. I retrieve my cell phone from my nightstand. I hesitantly sit on my bed and unlock it. I open my contacts, find the name I'm looking for, and hit the call button. It rings two times before a voice comes from the other end.

"Will?"

"Can you meet?"

"On my way, text me the address," Sage replies hastily.

I hung up the phone then sent the text with my address. For the first time, I think about how nothing that just happened makes sense. It's not physically possible. How was she in my dream? Am I still dreaming, for that matter? I have to be because no human can enter another person's mind, let alone dream.

That's it. I'm still dreaming. I have to be.

An hour later, I'm still sitting on my steps waiting for Sage to get here. I hear a car approaching before I see it pass my house. Anxious, I jump up and begin to pace the front deck. A minute later, I hear another car approaching. I focus on the black Challenger as it slows and pulls up to the curb. In a matter of seconds, the vehicle is parked and Sage jumps out, heading up my sidewalk.

Before I can stop myself, I blurt out, "How did you get into my dream? Am I still dreaming?"

"You are awake right now. I have a lot to tell you and not a lot of time to do it, but for me to tell you what needs to be said, you need to have an open mind. Can you do that?"

My following words come out more bitter and sarcastic than I mean them to. "Sure. Mind is open, now start filling in the blanks because right now, this feels like a dream."

"We're called dream walkers. There's a lot involved with what a dream walker is, what we can do, and who you really are."

"Meaning?"

"Listen, Will, I have a lot to tell you, as I said, and not much time to do it, so I need you to sit back and listen and be quiet, as hard as I know that is for you to do."

I open my mouth to shoot some snotty comment back at her but think better of it. Answers are more important right now. So instead, I just nod my head in agreement.

"Thank you." She takes a few more steps towards me. "I find the best place to start is the beginning. I learned what I was from a young age, and being someone who likes to have all the facts, I've done a lot of research over the years about what we are, but I'm still not a hundred percent sure what it all means. But the first thing you should know is there aren't too many like us out there, and even though we are dream walkers, it's hard to say what kind we are."

"What kind?"

As soon as the words leave my mouth, I think twice, and the look on her face only makes me wish I didn't say a word.

"Like I was saying, there are a few different kinds of dream walkers. One kind is the lowest level which can only change their dreams to something they want to see or happen while in the dreamscape. The next level can do that, but they can also dream walk into other people's dreams and come and go as they please. When they are in the person's dream, no one even notices they are there, kind of like a fly on the wall being able to listen and watch all the dirty secrets unfold." She pauses for a moment to wink at me. "The last kind of dream walker hasn't been around for thousands of years, so the bloodline more than likely dried up. That kind of dream walker's powers are unlimited from what I read about them as they are a direct descendant from the original line of walkers which had strong witch blood ties in their family. They not only can do everything I've already said, but they can also create their world, a dreamscape all of their own making, like an alternate reality to live in. They can take things back and forth with them from the dream world to our world and vice versa. Even things that are alive, like animals and humans."

I know I shouldn't ask, but I have so many questions. I know asking one is going to get a look, so I ask the main two at the front of my mind.

"What do you mean by, they can take things back and forth with them in between the worlds? You also mentioned that the person dreaming can't see the dream walker who enters their mind, so how was I able to see you?"

Surprisingly, she doesn't look annoyed when she answers.

"The reason you could see me in your dream is because you are a dream walker like me. Otherwise, I would have gone unnoticed. As for your other question, say you are the highest-level dream walker, and you wanted me to go into your dream with you. You would only have to hold onto me until you fell asleep, and then I would come along for the ride. The same thing would be for me to return to the real world. You just need to hold onto me. But this kind of dream walker hasn't existed for hundreds of years. But…"

She stops and begins to look around us, almost like she's expecting to see someone watching us from the bushes or something.

I realize she isn't going to start talking again, so I ask, "But what?"

Her attention turns back to me, her voice at a whisper now. "I'm sorry. The next part is what I'm worried about discussing. Can we maybe go sit in my car?"

"Um, sure, but my couch might be a little more comfortable."

"I don't know if it's safe."

I decide not to ask what she means by that. Instead, I gesture towards her car. Once we are sitting inside, she turns the radio on low before continuing the conversation.

"There is this organization that is looking for people like us. They are everywhere and nowhere at the same time. They are the reason there are so little of us left. They want to recruit and train us. I don't know the whole picture, but I know it's to bring back this big bad and, I guess, to be his army or something of that sort."

"What do you mean? And how do you know about this organization if they are nowhere, as you say?"

"I know because they found me a few years ago. They took me and trained me, but when I wanted to leave, they wouldn't let me. I had to escape, and since then, I've been in hiding and never stayed in one place for too long."

"So, you're telling me this group just took you? What about your family?"

I see the hurt in her eyes before she replies, "My family isn't around." She pauses, turning to look back at me. "Will, don't you realize how much danger you could be in, especially since you don't know how to use your power yet? You have no way of cloaking yourself from them and protecting yourself. You need to learn fast."

"Well, duh. I didn't even know what a dream walker was, let alone that they existed, or I was one. However, I think you might be right about needing to learn how to shield my dreams or whatever."

I think back to all the creepy dreams I've had the last few months and feeling like I'm being watched, and the encounters with Morpheus. What if he's real? What if he works with this organization she's talking about? He did say his followers where searching for me.

Worry creeps into her expression. "Will, what aren't you telling me?"

"Well, in some of my dreams lately, there have been these men following me, but I always seem to wake up before they reach me. What did you mean by, your family isn't around? You're seventeen years old. Where else would they be?"

She shakes her head violently, "Don't worry about me. You need to worry about yourself. From what you're telling me, that's the Company. They must already know about you, which means you're not safe. Your home isn't safe, and your mother and friends aren't safe, either."

Everything I've been experiencing in my dreams is real? How is this even possible? Those men who were following me and Morpheus were real? What do they want from me?

I remember the conversations with Morpheus, and suddenly I'm on high alert.

"None of this makes any sense. Why would they want me? How would they even know about me when I don't even know anything about me? And why would anyone be in danger if they only want to train me? What would my family and friends have to do with anything?"

"We need to drive for a bit while we talk some more. Is that OK with you?"

I nod, and she takes off down the road faster than I would like.

"The Company seems to have a way to track people of our kind. They use this computer program to track our ancestors, who were also walkers, then track us and test us to see if we have the gene. That's how they found me, but I already knew about my power by the time they did. But, just like you, I didn't know how to use them properly or what I was capable of. The only good thing that came out of it was that they taught me how to use my power faster and better than I could have learned on my own. But, when they wouldn't let me leave, I did some digging of my own."

The way she says the last sentence makes me uneasy. "What did you find?"

"They want to use our power to bring someone back from the dead, someone evil."

My mind travels back to my dreams, of the dark emptiness haunting me. Of Morpheus.

"How would that be possible, even with our powers?"

"Oh, yeah, sorry. Forgot about that part. The highest level of walker can bring people back from the dead, but there's a catch. You can't bring anyone back, only other walkers. When a walker dies, our soul is taken to the dream realm, another plane of existence, I guess you could say. For us, this is our purgatory. We sit there until we choose to move on to be judged. Some wait a long time. If our soul is still there, then the ultimate dream walker can find us and bring us back, but I'm sure it comes with a price, and I don't know what it is. Magic always comes with a price."

Every part of me grows numb.

West.

"Will, this is no joke. You need to learn how to cloak yourself from them and fast. From the sound of your dream, they might not know who you are yet or where you live because they would have come for you by now. So, you need to start being more careful with your dreams."

My anger boils over as I shout, "How am I supposed to do that when I don't even know what I am? I don't know how this works, how to turn it on or off like you do." I realize my words came out harsher than I meant, and I drop my head. "I'm sorry. I didn't mean to snap. I'm just overwhelmed and have so many questions. I mean, like my life wasn't already crazy enough. I haven't even been able to sort through my shit-show of a life as is, and now this gets piled on, and I don't know what to do with it."

"It's going to take some time, but I promise it will all make sense once we are done. The most important thing right now is to make sure we keep you safe so I can teach you. Teaching you is how we will learn what level you are."

I release a long sigh as I close my eyes. "So, how do I protect myself?"

"There are some herbs and stones I brought with me. I'll walk you through what to do with them every night before you go to sleep. But, what to do once you fall asleep is the most important. You need to close your eyes, clear your mind, and focus. Imagine a shield around your body, then focus on pushing that shield out as far as you can. You will feel it and see it, and you will see how far it goes. That is your primary protection. You need to do this every time you fall asleep. Then, if they still find you in your dream, you close your eyes again, take a deep breath, and envision yourself as if you aren't there. You're a cloud of smoke; you're invisible, and to them, you will become just that."

"But how will I know it works?"

"We will do a test run once we are both asleep. But I need to get you home now, then go and make some arrangements. We can get together soon, and I promise I'll fill you in on what I can."

"Sage, you said before you didn't know what the Company was training you for."

She nods.

"But then you said they are trying to bring this person back."

Another nod.

"I guess what I'm trying to ask is, who is he? And if they are training you, is it to bring him back? Or for something more? You said you didn't know what you were being trained to do, so I'm confused."

"As far as I know, the person they want is trapped in a dreamscape, like the one I told you we go to when we die. I know he's not someone we want to let out. And regarding the purpose behind the training, anyone who isn't the ultimate walker, I think they plan on having as this person's backup, maybe? I'm not too sure, honestly. All I know is it's nothing good."

"Is that what's been happening with all those disappearances the last year? All those families disappearing from their homes?"

She nods with a sad expression.

Right before West was killed, there were families worldwide that kept going missing. It was all over the news. No one could explain it. The family would be inside for the night, doors locked, and then a few days would pass, and people would notice they weren't showing up at their work and school and send someone to look for them. Eventually, the cops broke down doors to find no one home, but that a struggle had taken place. The thing that stumped everyone was that the deadbolts were on all the doors. Everything was still locked from the inside. So how did they leave?

Before long, we return to my house.

I reach for the door handle before turning to face her once more. "It wasn't a coincidence, was it?"

"What?"

"Us meeting."

"Nothing's ever a coincidence in life," she whispers.

I sigh as I exit the car and walk up the drive. I know there's something she isn't sharing, and my nerves tell me it's something I need to find out, and soon.

I hear Sage say from her car, "And don't think we won't be talking about that dream of yours."

I turn around to see a smirk on her face as she takes off down the road, leaving my heart in my throat. *Why couldn't she have dream-walked into a dream where I wasn't kissing her like a lovesick teenage boy?*

I crawl into my bed, exhausted but more afraid than ever to go to sleep.

Chapter 9

With all the changes in my life, there has only been a handful of people I would usually confide in. My brother West, but he's gone. My mother, but I don't think this is the best time to confide in her. Then there's Trey and Thea. Trey is nice because, well, he's a guy, but right now, I think Thea is the best option.

I flip through my contacts until I find her name.

I know you probably have plans since it's Sunday, but I was hoping we could talk.

I sit patiently on my bed, staring at my phone, until the screen flashes.

On my way.

A smile comes to my face. Thea has always been there for me when it counts. All I ever had to do was ask. Knowing this is what has me so confused. Why was she not there for me when everything happened with my family? It was the three of us all my life, and there's nothing we went through alone. Yet, there I was, alone. But why? What changed for them to walk away so abruptly only to return now, as my dreams turn darker? Could it be a coincidence, or are they hiding something from me, too?

I shake my head violently.

Smiling, I whisper to myself, "Get a grip, Will."

Thea has never lied to me, but then again, neither has my mother. So, why did I believe Morpheus when he said my family was hiding the truth from me? Well, I know my mother, and I can see from her actions and changes with the simplest of things that something is off. I can't say she's lying to me, but I know something is different. If my mother is hiding something, it's possible Thea could be too. The thought of the remaining people in my life keeping something important from me sets my nerves ablaze.

It's one thing when someone you aren't close to and don't trust with your life lies to you, but when it's someone you've never once doubted who's keeping something from you, that's a lot worse. I know I need answers, but right now, I just need someone in my corner telling me I'm not crazy.

* * *

"What's going on, Will?"

Sitting on my living room couch, I've never felt so out of place. Where do I even begin? Do I tell her about the dream walker stuff? That I think my mother is lying to me? About my dreams?

No, I think I'll start with something simpler.

"You know me better than most people, Thea. I've been feeling…."

"Not yourself," she says.

"I guess that's one way of putting it."

I rub the back of my neck nervously. Thea and I have talked about other girls I've been into or had a fling with, just like she's told me about guys. So why do I feel so uncomfortable talking about it now?

"Will?"

"Sorry, I'm just trying to figure out how to word it."

She leans back against the couch, waiting patiently for me to speak. That's the best thing about her. She never pushes or rushes me. She's patient and always understanding. I'm lucky to have someone like her as a best friend, someone I can tell anything and trust with my life. Dreams or no dreams, I know I can trust her.

"I've been feeling weird around the new girl."

"Sage?"

"Yes. I'm, well, I find myself—"

I can't get the words out. Something has shifted between Thea and me, and even though I don't know for sure what the change is, I feel this is something

I shouldn't share with her. Not because I don't trust her, but it runs deeper than that.

"Attracted to her?" She whispers.

My eyes connect with hers, unsure of how to continue. But, despite the smile on her face, I can see in her eyes a pain she is trying to hide.

"Yeah. But I don't understand it."

"She's beautiful."

"Yes, but that's not it."

Giggling, she says, "What? You don't go for pretty girls anymore?"

The corner of my mouth turns up into a smile. "It's not that. I feel a pull towards her. Something I can't control."

Moving back to put more space between us, Thea looks at me with confusion in her eyes.

"What do you mean?"

I sigh. "I know when you have feelings for someone, you can't always control them, but this is something more. I barely know the girl, yet...."

We sit in silence for a moment until Thea breaks the tension.

"What?"

I close my eyes before replying, "When I'm not with her, I don't think about her, at least not in that way."

"And when you are with her?"

I open my eyes, turning my gaze back to her. "I think about crossing that friendship line."

"You mean—"

I cut her short, "Yeah."

I see sadness creeping into the lines of her face, knowing something I've said has gotten under her thick exterior. I only wish I knew what.

"OK, so you want to kiss her? I don't see what the problem is or why you feel something's wrong."

"Thea, when have you ever known me to move that fast with any girl or take an interest in one this quickly?"

"Well, when you put it that way, never. But you have had a few girlfriends," she says with a smirk.

"I'm being serious."

Her smile disappears. "I know. I'm sorry. I just don't know what you think could be wrong. Like, what are you asking me?"

I rub my hands over my face roughly. "I don't know. I just feel like something is off. The moment I bumped into her in the hall that day, I felt something shift, but I didn't know what. We'd seen each other plenty of times in passing the first half of the year, and I did notice her and couldn't help looking her way, but when our shoulders connected, it took my notice to a different level. Now, when I'm around her, that pull only gets stronger, and it makes no sense to me."

"You are of the male species. Maybe it's just that primal thing you guys tend to have."

"I'm not a pig, Thea."

Smiling, she mumbles, "I never said you were. But maybe this is normal."

I shake my head. "I don't think so."

"OK. Then what do you want to do about it?"

"I don't know. Maybe you're right. Maybe I'm crazy," I say with a chuckle.

"You're not crazy, but maybe I am."

I glance in her direction. "Why do you think that?"

"I can't help feeling this isn't the real reason you wanted me to come over. Is something else going on?"

You have no idea.

"Yes, I mean, no."

Thea places her hand on mine, "What?"

"A lot of things are changing. I learned something new about myself, and I don't know what to think about it."

Her eyes shift, but only for a moment, though it's long enough for me to see there's something she isn't telling me. Something my words made her realize.

"You can trust me, Will."

"I know. I'm just not ready to talk about it yet."

She nods. "OK, well, when you are, I'm here."

I smile at her before standing.

"Where are you going?"

"Sage is coming over soon."

The sadness returns to her eyes, but only for a moment before she stands as well.

"I guess all I can say is be careful. If you feel something is off, trust your instincts." She places her hand on the knob of the front door before saying over her shoulder, "I guess I'll see you tomorrow at school."

"Count on it."

Chapter 10

"You alone?" Sage asks quietly as she walks through the front door of my house.

"Yes. My mom won't be home from work for hours."

"Good."

She walks into the living room and throws down her goth-looking bag on the couch with sheer determination before turning back around to face me.

"Hope you're ready for a long sleep."

My eyes widen as I realize I'm wide awake. I ruffle the hair on the back of my head. "Honestly, I'm not tired."

She closes the distance between us. "Doesn't matter. I can teach you how to go in without wanting or needing to sleep."

I watch as she walks into the kitchen.

"Seems there's a lot we can do."

"You have no idea."

She opens the cabinet closest to the sink, inspecting the contents. Unable to find what she's looking for, she closes it and moves on to the next cabinet. I cross my arms and lean against the wall looking at her.

"Where are your cups?"

Standing up straight, I point at the cabinet next to the fridge.

She smiles at me before pulling the door open to find her prize. "Thank you."

"I need you to fill in some blanks here, Sage."

"I will. Just let me get some fluid in me, and we are off to the races."

She turns on the kitchen faucet, filling her glass to the top. I watch as she places it to her lips and chugs it greedily. Water escaping from the sides of her mouth onto her white blouse causes me to avert my eyes as her black bra becomes visible through her shirt. She either doesn't notice or doesn't care as she finishes the glass, wipes her face on the back of her sleeve, and cleans the glass. Then, placing it in the strainer, she faces me with a grin.

"Where's your bedroom, stud?"

My heart leaps in my chest as she places her hands on her hips, only giving me a better view of her soaked top. Before I can stop them, my eyes trail down until I'm looking at the wet spot, now seeing her tan cleavage through her clothes. If her bra were any smaller, I would have a full view of her breast. Heat takes place on my face as I look away.

"Like what you see, William?" She asked playfully.

I force myself to turn back to her, looking her in the eyes. "The name's Will, not William, and my room is this way."

I take off down the hall and don't stop until I'm standing in front of my bed. I don't hear Sage behind me, and I don't know she's even there until her hand is on my back, and she leans in close, whispering in my ear.

"You didn't answer my question, *Will.*"

She says my name in a tone that sends chills coursing through me, and I fight to control the reaction my body has to her being this close. She moves around till she's standing in front of me, our bodies so close they are touching. My heart pounds so loud I can hear it in my ears. Her charcoal eyes look into my sapphire ones with a desire I'm not used to seeing.

"I saw your dream, Will. You don't have to be shy with me."

I feel my throat close at her words. I'm still feeling the pull towards her, but for some reason, it's not as intense as it used to be, which is a good thing considering the situation right now. However, it's only making things more confusing. I know I feel something for her, who wouldn't? She's beautiful, smart, sassy and determined.

But sex isn't something to ever take lightly, and for a woman, it's more important, at least, that's what my mother taught me. As uncomfortable as I was talking with my mother, I'm glad I did. It allowed me to understand women a lot more than I'm sure most men do. From what I know about Sage, she's alone–no family–and I'm guessing she's on the run, making her life lonely. Maybe I'm the first dream walker she's met, I don't know. But I know what it's like to feel alone and do anything to be close to someone, but I won't do that. Not here and not now.

I like Sage, and the pull I feel towards her is strong. As badly as I want to act on it, I know now isn't the time. There are more critical things to focus on, like staying alive. If we ever cross that bridge, I want it to be after we've had time to get to know each other a little better and after I can show her I'm not like the other guys I'm guessing she's used to. I won't be with her and then disappear. When I'm with someone, I'm with them.

"Are you going to come sit next to me?" Sage asks.

I sigh as I take my place on my bed and face her. "Sage."

She moves closer. "Yes?"

"I like you. I'm sure you already know that."

She giggles lightly. "Duh."

"I also know that from what you said, there are more important things for us to focus on right now. I can tell you're afraid of whoever these people are, and I know what it's like to want to lose yourself in something, so you don't feel the fear anymore, but I can't do that. I need answers, and I need to learn how to use this power. Not only to protect me and my family and friends, but hopefully to be some kind of help and protection for you." I lean closer to her as I take a deep breath. "I don't want you to have to run anymore. I want to help you. Please, let me do that."

Her expression changes. Her once fake seductive nature turns, only to reveal her genuine emotions. I see the fear etched into every line of her face, mixing with uncertainty. I know we barely know each other, but I mean everything I just said. I want to help her. No one deserves to live their lives afraid and on the run, bouncing from place to place. Especially not someone as young as Sage. I study her, and for the first time, fear finds me. I could quickly become her. If I don't learn how to use this power and figure out who these people are and how to stop them, then I will be in the same place she is soon.

"Sage."

"I want you to know something."

"What's that?" I ask curiously.

"I do like to lose myself in different things, to get my life off my mind for a little bit, but," her eyes turn soft as the corner of her mouth lifts higher in a slight smirk, "I would be lying if I didn't say I feel something with you, Will. Something I haven't in a long time. You confuse and overwhelm me in ways I'm not used to. That's why I tried to be so cruel at school when we first met. I couldn't afford the distraction."

The chuckle escapes my lips before I can stop it. "Me? A distraction?"

As much as I know the way I'm feeling doesn't add up, I can't deny that I don't feel something for her because I do. I think about kissing her lately when we aren't around each other or wonder what she could be up to but I know how strong I feel when we are around each other, like now, doesn't add up and that's what makes me nervous.

Her cheeks turn red as she averts her eyes. "Yes. You're very handsome, smart and kind. I've noticed. Any girl would be stupid to look the other way."

My eyes widen in surprise at her words.

"I…" I rub at the back of my neck nervously. "I've never really seen myself that way, I guess."

"We normally never picture ourselves the way others do. But," her eyes lock mine in place, "I see you, Will."

And just like that, I'm falling once more. I want so much to touch her, hold her close and tell her everything will be alright, that we will figure things out so she can stop running. But I know I can't make those promises, not yet.

"Before I change the subject, I want you to know I see you, too."

Sage's eyes shine at my words before her cheeks turn red once more, and she moves back on the bed with a smile.

"Well, then. Now that we got that out of the way." She giggles. "It's time to see who you really are, Will Walker."

It takes Sage a good half hour to explain how we can get into our dreams without being ready to sleep. Then she gave me a tea mixture she made.

When I ask what's in it, she laughs and tells me it's chamomile. I drink the contents of the mug, and we lay on the bed next to one another.

"Ready?" She asks.

"Ready," I reply.

She told me all I had to do was clear my mind and relax. Think of falling to sleep, and just like that, I should fall into it. It takes me a couple of tries, but then I feel my body becoming weightless as my mind wanders and I fall into the darkness.

Floating.

Tingly.

The thick air around me makes it hard to breathe until my body rests against something firm, and the air becomes thin once more. I peel my eyes open to see Sage standing over me with a grin on her face, offering me her hand.

"Well done. Not bad for the first time."

I take her hand, stand, and brush the dirt off my clothes as I look around. "Where are we?"

"You tell me. It's your dream."

I glance around, seeing only trees. My body reacts without thought, and the next thing I know, I'm walking through the trees. I hear Sage following behind me as I pick up the pace until I reach a clearing, and my heart stops.

"Not here," I whisper. "Anywhere but here."

Sage reaches my side, glancing around before her eyes land on me. "What? Where are we?"

I take an involuntary step forward. "This is where it happened."

"Where what happened?"

My eyes sting as tears fight to come to the surface, but I blink them back into their home. I won't do this, not here. I try to form words, but nothing comes out.

Sage gasps behind me as her hand rests over her mouth. Her eyes are sad as they meet mine.

"This is where..." She trails off.

Nothing else needs to be said as I nod, knowing she knows where we are.

I don't remember much from that day, everything is still mostly a blur, but the one thing I can never erase from my mind is where it all happened. Here, in this place, is where I lost my best friend, my life, and my fight all at once. This is where I became a frightened child once again.

This is where my brother died.

Sage places her hand in mine. "Maybe…" She looks off to the body of water in front of us. "Maybe you brought us here for a reason."

"And what might that be?" I ask harshly.

"You need to deal with this, Will. I know it's not fair or easy, but until you do, your mind will continue to be a fraction of what it really is."

My glare falls on her. "What does that mean?"

"Right now, your mind is filled, shattered, and broken with what happened here. It's consuming you, and because of that, your powers won't work as well as they would otherwise. Your powers are linked to your emotions." She squeezes my hand lightly. "If you want to be able to learn, to grow in them and become strong enough to face what's coming our way, then this is something you need to deal with."

I look back at the body of water in front of me as I release a long breath. "I wish it was that easy. I don't even remember what happened."

Sage moves to stand in front of me. "Maybe I can help with that."

Our eyes lock once more, sending my heart into overdrive. "How?"

"First, we need to unlock your mind and your gifts."

"I'm all ears."

"OK. Let's start with something simple."

She pulls me over to a shady area next to the body of water. It takes everything in me not to run in the opposite direction. Being this close to the water makes it hard to breathe. I need to get a grip.

"Close your eyes."

I sigh and do as she says.

"I want you to envision the scenery around us shifting, changing into something else. I want you to take us to a different place. Think about the trees changing, the lake disappearing."

I inhale deeply through my nose, thinking about the world shifting, morphing into my front yard, willing us to be back home. I think about this for less than a minute when I hear Sage gasp, causing my eyes to open.

She's looking around us in surprise to see we are now outside my home. "Wow."

"You seem surprised?"

Her eyes lock on mine, and I'm unsure if what I'm seeing is hope or fear. "You could say that."

I take a slow step in her direction. "You said this is a level-one dream walker power. Being a dream walker, I should be able to do this, but I can't help feeling your surprise is for another reason."

She closes the distance between us. "Will, you did that in mere seconds."

"And?"

I don't understand what the big deal is. This is something I should be able to do. So why would it matter if I did it slower or not?

"It takes new walkers hours to shift even one thing in the dream to something else."

"Oh."

She smiles. "Yeah."

I toss my hair nervously with my hand. "Well, what can I say? I'm a fast learner."

"That has nothing to do with it. All I did was tell you what to think about. No other instructions were needed. You just did it."

"Again, I don't understand why that's a problem?"

She takes my hands in hers. "It's not. It only means you're stronger than either of us thought. I can only imagine if your mind wasn't shattered and filled with loss, what else you would be capable of."

The way she says it makes my blood run cold, and for the first time, I'm afraid of what I am. You would think hearing I had supernatural powers would be enough to scare anyone, but for some reason, when Sage first told me what I was, it felt...right. Like I knew deep down, I was unaware of some hidden thing inside me. I always felt out of place, but I chalked that up to being a teen in high school and going through all the changes every typical teen does.

Boy, I couldn't have been more wrong.

I've been afraid and worried for my family and friends since learning these men in my dreams are real, meaning that thing in the darkness might be real, which in and of itself is terrifying. But this is the first time I've been afraid of what I might be capable of.

I don't think I would be one of those people to turn to the dark side, but isn't that what everyone thinks?

"Will?"

"Sorry. I was…"

"Lost in thought."

"You could say that."

"A lot is changing for you, so I get feeling overwhelmed or even scared, but that's why I'm here. Let me help you."

"I'm worried."

She places her hand on my cheek trying to reassure me. "There are a lot of things to be worried about, but what are you thinking about at this moment?"

"I'm worried about who I could become because of this new power."

"As I told you before, you're kind and good. I don't see you turning to the dark side." Sage laughs.

"Even Superman turned evil a few times. Sometimes you have no control over it. Sometimes it's fate."

"Do you think that's what fate has in store for you?"

"It doesn't matter what I think. Fate is fate. In the end, it finds all of us."

"I don't think I think of fate like you do."

"And how's that?"

"I think we control our futures. We have free will to make our own decisions. Free will is a big thing with the man upstairs; I believe our lives are planned out, but our destination depends on our choices along the way. Nothing is set in stone."

"For our sake, I hope you're right because if this agency keeps finding people like us and taking them, what's to stop them from getting in our heads? From changing our values and beliefs and turning us into something we always feared? I mean, if they can find us and do all these things you've mentioned,

I wouldn't put it past them to add brainwashing or reprogramming to that list."

Sage sighs before she turns to walk away. "They are very dangerous, and like I've said, you're smarter than you let people believe. I've heard about their end game and how they plan on achieving it." She looks over her shoulder at me. "That's why we need to be ready for them." Now on my front step, she turns to face me. "Don't be afraid of how easily these powers come to you, Will. I believe there is a reason I ended up here and at your school, and I believe there is a bigger reason why you are a dream walker." She smiles widely before taking a seat on the chair outside my front door. "Who knows? Maybe you're the one they are looking for, and just maybe, you will be the one to take them down."

"Then I guess we better find out." I sit in the unoccupied chair next to her. "What's next?"

"Easy there, slick. All in good time. What you just achieved, and how fast, is a great start for now. Just take a moment to breathe it all in. A lot is changing and fast, and if you don't take the time to let it sink in, your mind will be worse off than it already is."

I shift uncomfortably in my seat. "I can rest later. Right now, we need answers. We need to know how strong I am, so do what you came here to do. Teach me."

Sage leans back in her chair and looks at me with surprise and what seems to be admiration. "OK, then. Let's test your strength." She leans in close to me, "I want you to focus on your hands."

I look down at them.

"Feel them. Make every fiber of your being know they are there. Focus only on them."

I nod.

"Now imagine them disappearing slowly before your eyes. One minute they are solid objects, and the next, you see through them like they are no longer a part of your body. Once you think that, I want you to shift your mind and imagine everyone around you not seeing your hands. They are invisible to everyone looking at you, but you can still see them, still feel

79

them."

I focus on my hands, removing everything else from my mind but this one task. I feel the sweat forming on my forehead as I release a breath, almost panting.

"Breath in slow. It's not as easy as it sounds. It will take a few tries, and you might not be able to do it even then. It's different than becoming invisible to the Company. But, as I mentioned earlier, that is more like you tapping into their mind and making yourself unseen. This is you physically making yourself invisible. Slowing, making each body part transparent."

The sweat moves down the length of my cheek as I move my attention to Sage, "How long did it take you to do this?"

A small smile spreads over her face. "A few hours, but if I'm being honest, I was already pretty in tune with my powers and strength, whereas you're just starting."

"When you finally were able to do it, what did you do differently? Maybe if you told me, I could use that and get it quicker."

Shrugging, she says, "It's worth a try. For me, I had to close everything around me out. The noises, colors, everything. I only focused on making myself invisible, and nothing else mattered. It took me a while to clear out my mind, but once I did, presto, invisible girl," giggling, she shifts in her chair, "the more I did it, the easier it became, and I could do it without closing the world around me out."

I did as she said and closed everything around me out. Ten minutes pass, then twenty, and just as I'm about to give up from the frustration and exhaustion, I look down at my hands as they begin to shift. One minute, they are solid, and the next, I can see my white shoes through them. Then, I refocus and push the transparency of my hands outward, making them visible to me once more but hopefully making them disappear before Sage.

I hear her suck in a breath as she moves away from me. "Will?"

"Did it work?"

She laughs. "A little too well, I think."

"What do you mean?" I ask nervously.

"I mean, not only did your hands disappear, but I can no longer see you."

"Like, all of me?"

She nods with a huge smile. "I want to try one more thing."

"OK."

"I want you to focus now like you did before, but instead, I want you to imagine what it would be like if I couldn't see or hear you. I want you to think about making it like you weren't here at all to anyone but yourself. Give yourself a minute, then say something to me. If I don't answer back, then I can't hear you, either. If this works, to shift back, close your eyes and picture your being–your hands, your face, your voice–all coming back to the surface, like it was submerged underwater. Focus on being seen and heard again."

"OK."

Focusing on closing out everything around me once more, I do as she says, and I feel a shift in the atmosphere around me, almost like an invisible bubble forming around my body. I open my eyes and take in a deep breath before standing from my seat and moving behind Sage.

"Can you hear me?"

She doesn't move.

I clap my hands together right behind her head.

Still nothing.

Wow. This is amazing. How is this even possible? How did I make it to almost eighteen years of age without knowing I had these powers, let alone going this long without them surfacing? Something isn't right. I close my eyes and imagine the bubble popping around me.

"Sage."

She jumps in her seat before turning around to look at me in surprise. "Wow. It worked."

"How old were you when your powers manifested?"

"I was around six, I think. Why?"

I begin to pace the porch. "Something's not right about this."

"What do you mean?"

I stop and look her in the eyes, seeing panic that matches my own.

"Why am I only now experiencing this change? Why did it take so long for me to come into these powers or this gift?"

Realization becomes clear in her eyes. "I honestly didn't think about that."

"On average, what age do dream walkers learn they are dream walkers?"

"I've never met anyone over the age of ten who didn't already know."

I release a long breath hoping it will take the feeling of dread and panic along with it. "That's what I was afraid of. Would my parents have known what I am?"

I'm afraid of her answer, but I know I need it. My mother has never lied to me a day in my life, and the thought of her keeping something this big from me has me worried. Not because I can't trust her, but because I know there was an excellent reason if she did. Maybe now I'm right in the middle of everything she tried so hard to hide and protect me from.

"Yes. This gift runs in our bloodline, so either one or both of your parents would have to have been a walker. But up until our recent generation, the power of the dream walkers has been limited. They couldn't do much, but for some reason, now the powers are back in full force with us."

"Why is that?"

She shakes her head, but I can see in her eyes there's something she isn't saying.

"I don't know for sure. I heard talk about the agency taking people who had the gene and running experiments on them to increase the power in their bloodlines."

"Meaning their children would be more powerful than they were." I rub my face violently.

"Exactly."

"I think I need to talk to my mom about this."

She nods. "I think that's a good idea. Just be careful."

"Why?"

"Because maybe she doesn't know anything about it. Maybe your father carried the gene."

I nod in understanding. So much for my life going back to normal. I finally reconnected with my friends and started to feel a little like my old self, and now this. There's one thing I know for sure: there's no going back now.

"Will?"

"Yeah?"

"Doing what you did just now makes you a level two dream walker and the strongest I've encountered. I'm worried if we don't keep this training going, the Company will find you, and if they do, I'm worried about what they will do."

"Me too."

"I know you want to talk to your mom, but I think we need to do a few more things before we wake up."

I nod. "I agree. Let's do it."

"I want you to envision your ideal place of peace, and I want you to bring it to life here in your dream. I want you to take this world and morph it into the place in your mind."

I rub my hands together, taking a deep breath. "Here goes nothing."

I think back to where my family and I were our happiest. The scenery was so beautiful, anyone could get swept away by it. The trees were taller than a double-decker home with no roads for miles, as a simple dirt path was all you used to drive your car until you stumbled upon the main roads. A place of life, nature, and the sounds of peace as birds chirping filled the air. This was a place where peace engulfed every fiber of your being, and you felt untouchable to the outside world. A place I would do anything to return to.

I open my eyes to find nothing has changed.

"It's OK. As I said, it takes time." Sage says encouragingly.

I sigh before closing my eyes once more. *I will get this. I have to get this.* I focus on everything again, trying harder to bring my memory to life. Sweat forms on my back, and I shiver as it runs down my spine. I open my eyes once again to see that nothing has changed. Exhausted, I place my hands on my knees, taking in deep breaths. I feel Sage's hand on my shoulder.

"It's OK. We can take a break."

"No." I stand up straight before continuing, "I need to get this. I need to learn as fast as I can. For all of our sake."

Sage nods in understanding and agreement as she moves back, giving me some space. I clear my mind and think only of the place I wish to recreate.

Nothing and no one else enters my mind. Sweat forms on my brow as I begin to envision the body of water that was half a mile away from our home when I hear Sage gasp. I open my eyes, unsure of what I'll find. But, as my gaze takes in the scene around me, my heart stops in my chest as my breath catches in my throat.

"I did it," I whisper.

"Will."

I want to answer her, but instead, I find myself taking a few steps deeper into the woods I have missed for so long.

"Will," Sage says from beside me once more.

I feel lost inside this moment as it takes me back to a happier time with my family and life in general. A time before our family unit was shattered and broken, before my father abandoned our family. My mother and I have always been closer than my father and I, but we were still close. My dad, brother, and I would go on a monthly weekend hiking trip for us to bond, and I have a lot of great memories with my father, but after West died and dad took off, he took all those memories with him. Now, standing in his place is an empty void. The only person I've had this past year is my mother, and our bond has strengthened in a way that can never be broken. If it weren't for her, I wouldn't be here. I would have lost myself in the darkness of my grief, but I made myself strong for her, and we were there for each other, as we've always been.

Looking around these woods, one thought alone fills my mind.

"I need to talk to my mother."

Sage places her hand on my arm. "Will."

My mind can't focus on anything other than the obvious right now as I glance at her.

"I think you're who they've been searching for." She stares into the woods. "If you can do this, I have no doubt you'll be able to summon a force field around you, maybe even travel back in time or manifest your powers in the awake world. No one has ever learned as fast as you have."

I turn back to gaze into the distance of my childhood home as fear sinks its fangs deep into my flesh. There's no escaping this now. Fate has a funny way of letting you know it's not done with you.

Chapter 11

S age didn't let me leave the dream right away, not before we had perfected my shield and invisibility. She also started to teach me to manipulate the dream world more. Like how to take one part and change it into something else I wanted in the scene. She wants to work on my dreamscape, to see if I can create my world, make a place that's entirely my design. She says it's the one place I'll be able to hide from the Company.

My thoughts end as I hear my mom in the kitchen. When I finally came out of the dreamscape last night, my mother was fast asleep, and I didn't want to wake her. I know we need to talk, and soon, but Sage will be here any moment, so I decide the best course of action, for now, is to act as if nothing has changed.

"Hey, Mom."

"I was wondering where you've been lately. I haven't seen you much since you started school. Although, I guess that's a good thing. You've been hanging out with Trey and Thea?"

Not too sure if I should tell her about Sage yet because then I would have to tell her about the other stuff too, and right now isn't the time to open that can of worms. "Yeah."

"That's great, honey. I'm glad you're getting together with your friends again. I was beginning to get a little worried about you. No kid your age should be at home all the time with their mom as their best friend."

"Who said you were my best friend?" I ask playfully.

"You're right," she replies as she places her finger on her chin. "I guess I just assumed since we would hang out every night and you would tell me things about your life. Like how you feel about Thea and how she gives you the...what did you call it? The–"

I throw my hands up in the air with a laugh. "Whoa, Mom. Those things were told to you in confidence, and the mother code means they are never to be spoken aloud again."

She begins laughing. "I missed you, Will."

I know those words hold more than she's letting on. What she means is she missed her son, the one she had before our lives were turned upside down. She misses the carefree, go-getter, happy son that was all about family, friends, school and art. The "good kid," I guess you could say.

"Missed you too, Mom. Maybe we can do a movie tonight? Do you have to go to work?"

"Nope, I'm all yours."

I turn to grab my jacket and head for the front door. "Awesome. I'll be home in a few hours. You pick the movie for tonight."

"See you then, be careful."

* * *

"Hey, Walker," Sage shouts even though she's practically standing right next to me.

"Calling me by my last name now?"

"Yup, figured it sounds better. Plus, Walker is a walker."

"Whatever you say." I laugh.

"Are you ready for this? It's going to take a lot of energy for your first time."

"Yeah, I'm ready."

"You didn't sleep much after I left, right?"

I shake my head. "Nope, did just as you said. Plus, after everything I learned about myself and my life, I don't think I could have slept even if I tried."

We walk inside her house, and the first thing I notice is how big and roomy it is. We walk into the back hallway until we come to a door. She pushes it open and reveals what must be her bedroom. The colors black, purple, and lavender pop out everywhere.

"OK, so lay down."

"Where?"

"On the bed, silly."

I move to stand next to her bed. Looking down at it, my body freezes. Being in my bed was one thing, but I'm finding it hard getting into a bed that isn't mine and with someone of the opposite sex. My bed was hard but this causes me to stop dead with uncertainty, like I'm about to cross a line of some sort. A bed is where we spend most of our time, and I find it a personal space, so laying down in hers is making me nervous. Or maybe it's what my mother brought up this morning. I laugh to myself at the memory.

"You gonna lay down or what?"

"Yeah, sorry."

Sage smiles, and it's almost like she knows what I'm thinking, which makes me feel even more uneasy. She already knows I'm into her, so being in this situation is a little unorthodox to me. She pats the area on the bed next to her as she looks at me with a questioning smile, causing me to look away as I sit beside her. She lays down once I sit and looks at me in a way to let me know to do the same. Without another word, I do. She places her hand next to mine, opening it for me to take. Without a word, I take her hand in mine. She smiles before turning her attention to the ceiling, closing her eyes.

I copy her motions.

"Clear your mind and think of what you want to dream about, what you want your world to look like."

* * *

A light breeze brushes my hot skin, causing me to open my eyes revealing trees in every direction. Spruce, pine, weeping willows surround me at every turn. Just like I imagined. To my right lies a river, and in the distance, I can see a waterfall. I turn to my left to find Sage looking around in awe. It took longer than I would have liked to pull us into the realm and shape what I was thinking about, but this view is more than worth it.

"What do you think?" I ask, turning to look back at Sage.

"It's beautiful."

My instincts take over my mind as the thought of touching and kissing her flashes behind my eyes. Her beautiful long hair is hugging her body, no makeup on, her skin untouched; she's never looked more inviting. She doesn't need all that extra stuff she puts on, and I would love to tell her that, but she's so headstrong and independent. I know telling her wouldn't make a difference anyway or worst case she would laugh in my face thinking I'm lying about how beautiful she is, she's just that kind of girl.

The way I've felt about our situation the last few weeks has shifted. What was once uncertainty about the pull towards her has turned into appreciation for her help and teaching me the basics of who I really am. Without her patience and time to teach me these things my family and I would be caught in the red light and unprotected. Everything she's done for me has been selfless which only caused me to open my eyes to what's really in front of me. Thea will always have a place in my heart and life but there is a reason I've never gone there and Sage is here, in front of me, being everything I could ever ask for in a partner.

She turns to find my eyes on her, causing her to blush. I move closer to her, taking her hand in mine as my other hand brushes the hair from her face. I slowly tip my head down to hers until our lips connect. Soft, safe, unsure. She removes her hand from mine and places it on my back, pulling me closer until our bodies are touching. Then, just as quickly, she's moving away again.

"Sage?"

"We really should keep training, no time to waste."

She turns to walk away, and as much as I want to get to the bottom of what just happened, I know she is right. However, her reaction just now feels like it runs deeper than the reason she stated. I mean she wanted more than a kiss not too long ago. I shake my head, ignoring the questions forming in my mind as I step in the opposite direction.

"So, where do we start?"

"Well, you've done a great job at laying down the foundation, but what else do you want?"

"Meaning?"

"Animals? House?"

"Oh, I see what you mean."

She turns away from me before saying, "Think hard and imagine it. This is to be your place of escape. A home away from home. Everything you've wanted but never had, and things you once had, but no longer do."

I see my vision unfolding behind my eyelids. I focus harder than I ever have, and my body is protesting big time. I hear Sage's voice as I focus on creating this new realm.

"This place isn't like the dream realm. This is more like a hidden plain in our world, it's real, but it's yours. You can bring anyone you want here, and it's the safest place because the Company can't enter unless you bring them here. It's kind of like you created your world outside of reality, but also keep in mind, once you bring someone here, they can come and go whenever they want."

If this place I'm creating isn't a dreamscape and I can bring anyone here, that would mean my friends. I could keep them safe. It's good to know that I have this as a backup plan, at least.

"What do you see?" I hear her voice, but I don't answer. "Will?"

I open my eyes to see her looking off in the distance at what looks like a pack of large cats, and I smile.

"You didn't…"

Unsure of the alarm in her voice, I ask, "What?"

"You thought of lions? Are you crazy? Wish them away. *Hurry*!"

"Why?"

"Because you're new at this. You won't be able to control them! They eat meat, and we are meat. The difference between this world and our awakened state is nothing; they are the same."

"Meaning?"

"You get hurt here. You get hurt there. This is the one place you can bring your body with you, even though we didn't this time it's still the same. We die here then we are dead there. This isn't like a normal dream, Will."

Instead of doing what she says, I move to stand in front of her.

"What are you *doing*?"

"Trust me."

"Are you crazy? Do you have a death wish or something?"

"Just trust me."

I can feel her terror as the enormous cats move closer. The closest one is a lioness, and she's beautiful, just like I imagined. Her coloring isn't of a typical lion. Instead, she's brown, black, and white. The white and black are defined around her eyes, paws, and tail. Her mate is different shades of browns and white and around his eyes and paws are black. The cub behind them has a more vibrant color tone. A mix of orange, red, and brown runs through his coat. However, color isn't the only difference. I also envisioned them bigger than the typical lion. These cats are about seven feet tall.

Sage grabs my arm and the back of my shirt as the lions make it across the river. With two more strides, they will be right in front of me. Once they reach my side, they stop. They look back and forth at each other, then crouch, almost like they are going to pounce.

"*Will!*"

I close my eyes, waiting for the blow, thinking maybe Sage was right, that I've bitten off more than I can chew, but then I hear it. A voice I don't recognize.

"Why do you seem afraid?"

I force my eyes open to see the mother lion looking at me.

"Did you just talk?"

"You wished for us to be able to communicate with you, did you not?"

"Yes, but I didn't realize it would actually work," I say with a grin.

This is unreal.

"This is your world, Will. Anything you want, you can have." The mother lion looks around me till her eyes land on Sage, "And please tell your companion she doesn't need to fear us. We aren't going to hurt you."

Sage moves to stand next to me. "How did you do this?"

"I don't know. I just did what you told me to do."

She looks at me in amazement. "But no one has ever been able to do anything like this."

"I guess there is a first time for everything."

"Will, you're not understanding what I'm saying."

I look over at her, sure that my confusion is plain on my face. "You're right; I don't."

"Remember what I told you about the higher-level walkers?"

"Yes."

"Well, we already know you're one of them, but..."

Her pause causes me to sigh before I mumble, "I think you're going to have to spell it out for me, Sage."

She releases a long, annoyed sigh. "No one has been able to do this kind of thing, ever, from what I read."

"OK."

"What I'm trying to say is even the higher-level Walkers weren't known to be able to bring animals to life and domesticate and communicate with them. This is something else." She turns her attention to the lions for a moment, "So, if you can do this, what else can you do?"

I glance at our surroundings before turning back to her. "I don't know. I thought that's what we were supposed to figure out together."

"And we are, but..."

"But, what?"

"The Company. You are their main target. You are in more danger than I thought. I was hoping I was wrong about you being the one they want, but you're more powerful than they anticipated."

"I thought they wanted everyone like us? I mean, I know they are looking for someone like me, too, but they want all of us, don't they?"

"Yes, they want us for an army, but what they *really* want is to find you."

"I know. I remember. But that's what this training is for; to prepare us."

"Will, if they find you, I'm worried about what they will be able to do with your power. This doesn't just mean you're strong. You have powers that are beyond anything and anyone else. You can bring people back from the dead."

West.

"They will make you bring back Morpheus. That is why they want you."

92

"They can't make me do anything I don't want to do. You should know me enough by now to know at least that."

"I do, Will, but I also know the Company. They have a way of making you do things you never thought you would."

The hurt and fear on her face sends my heart to a stand still.

"I have nothing they can hold over me."

"You're wrong about that."

"Meaning?"

I see the wheels turning in her head before she says, "Meaning you still have friends and your Mom."

"I would never let anything happen to them," I say angrily.

"I know you wouldn't, but you might not have a choice in the matter. They will do whatever they need to in order to get to you. They've been searching for you for over a hundred years." Sadness takes over her features. "I'm sorry. I just want you to understand what this could mean for you. It won't be an easy road."

"I know, but I have faith that with your smarts and training, I know we can figure out how to take the Company down."

"I don't think there is a way to take them down. They are too big."

"There's always a way," I say, determined. "But for now, let's enjoy being here and in this moment. We can fight another day. Agreed?"

I can see the hesitation in her eyes, but she nods in agreement before a small smile emerges on her face.

I turn my attention back to the lions. "What are your names?"

"You already named us," the cub says.

Surprised, I say, looking at the lioness, "So that would make you Rain, your mate Bronx, and your cub Rox."

"Yes."

"This is intense."

Sage smiles. "Yes, but it's pretty cool."

My mind suddenly becomes very overwhelmed. So much in my life has changed this past year. One minute, I had a completely happy family, then in the blink of an eye, I lost half of them. Now I've been thrown into a world I never even knew existed. A world my family hid from me, and now I'm here playing catch up to be strong enough to protect the ones I love and hopefully put an end to the Company and get back to everyday life. Whatever that is.

"So, what do we do now?"

"We keep training," Sage replies.

I stand up from petting Rox, the youngest lion.

"What's next?"

"Focus on creating this place. They shouldn't be able to enter this world–no one should–without you bringing them here. "

My earlier thought pops into my head. "If that's the case, why can't I just bring everyone here to keep them safe for now?"

"It's not as simple as all that. If they aren't a walker, you need to share who you are with them, and then you need to prepare their minds for the change. If they don't have a strong mind, then they could get lost in this realm, become a part of it, so to speak."

"What does that mean?"

Her eyes look at me sadly, "It means they would become a part of this place, no longer truly themselves, and for that reason returning them to reality would be hard, if not impossible."

Rain's voice comes from behind me, "Do you think you could make us something to eat, please? This may not be your real world, but for us, it is. We need to breathe and eat just like you would in your reality."

I scratch at the back of my head, annoyed with myself. "Oh, I didn't think about that. Sorry."

I concentrate on making different kinds of animals for them to hunt and plants for them to eat. When I open my eyes, I see them running off into the distance after an antelope. I turn back to Sage, who is staring off into the distance. Looking contemplative.

"What's wrong?"

"Nothing."

I place my hand on her cheek. "No, something's wrong. I know we haven't known each other long, but I can tell when something's bothering you or on your mind."

I can see she's fighting hard with something before she says, "We can't do this." She removes my hand from her face, taking a step back.

"Can't do what?"

She peers up at me, sadness evident in her eyes. "Us."

I would be lying if I said I haven't been thinking about her or the possibility of *us.* She's intense, interesting, intelligent, strong, independent, beautiful, and she's totally saving my ass, teaching me all this. I haven't dated anyone in so long, and now, with everyone I know being in danger because of what I am, the feeling of being in a relationship right now feels weird, foreign, and wrong.

"What about us?"

"There can't be an us, Will."

"Why not?" The words come out before I can stop myself.

I agree with her on some level. Right now isn't the time for romantic entanglements, but it doesn't mean it wouldn't be nice to have someone there every step of the way. Someone to get close to and be your shoulder when it's needed. Someone in your corner to help you through all the tough choices. I would love that, and for Sage to be that person would be so easy. Not only because she knows what is now my deepest secret, but she also knows the danger and is strong enough to handle it and anything that comes our way.

"Because there just can't," she says as she turns away from me. "I'm not good for you. I'm only here to teach you what you need to know to protect yourself, and that's it."

"If you don't feel what I feel, then just tell me. I can take it."

She turns away from me again and looks into the forest.

"Sage."

"It's not that Will."

"Then what is it? I know right now isn't the best time for us to get involved, but it would still be nice to know what's going on in your head."

"There are things I'm not ready to talk about, but once I do, you're not going to like the person I am." Her eyes return to me. "So I'm saving us both the hurt that would come from this in the long run."

"Things you're not ready to talk about? OK, I get you don't want to talk about them right now. I understand. But I don't see anything changing the way I feel about you. You're amazing and if it wasn't for you I would never have learned the truth and how to use my powers so that I can protect everyone." I place my hand under her chin and lift her head to look back at me. "And I know you feel the same way. I've felt this pull, this connection with you since the day we met."

"It doesn't matter what I'm feeling. All that matters is what I know."

"And what's that?"

"Can we please just focus on the training for now? We don't have time for distractions."

"Is that what you think this is? A distraction? If anything, it's a reason to fight harder."

Sage releases a long sigh that sends a chill down my spine. *What is she hiding from me?* She was all for this before, but now that I want to see if there is something between us, she couldn't get further away from me.

"What's going on?"

She wraps her arms around herself as if she were cold. "Nothing."

"I may not have known you for very long, but I know when someone is lying to me or hiding something. So what is it?"

When she turns to face me, a small smile is spread across her face, but her eyes hold a different story. Filled with pain and fear, they lock with mine, and it takes everything in me not to move closer to her. To hold her and let her know everything will be all alright.

Our conversation ended there as the air between us turned thick. We trained for another hour or so before we left the dream world. When we returned to our world, or realm, whichever you prefer, we locked eyes before she got up from the bed without so much as a word.

Chapter 12

I walk through my front door, leaving the tension from today outside our home. As I cross the threshold, I feel lighter than I have in a long time. Like I can breathe. No longer is there a boulder sitting on my chest. But then, I hear it.

"Mom?" I whisper.

I move further into the hall of my childhood home, every step taking me closer to my mother's room and the sound of someone crying softly. Her door is cracked just enough for me to gaze through. I see her sitting in her comfy chair by the window. I strain my eyes to make out the object she's clinging to for dear life, seeing that it's one of my brother's beat-up t-shirts.

I rub at my neck nervously, knowing there's nothing I can do for her. Interrupting her to try to soothe her will only make matters worse. The best thing I can do is give her space. I turn away hesitantly before walking to my dark, cold bedroom. Seeing the clock only reading 3:15 p.m., I know dinner won't be ready for another two hours. Just enough time for a nap.

I jump on my bed, forcing all the dark thoughts from my mind as I close my eyes. But, to my surprise, it takes no time at all before I fall into the deep abyss of sleep.

* * *

The cool breeze seeps into my bones, causing a chill to run over my spine as I shiver. I rise from the ground, peering into the darkness around me. As hard as I try, I can't see anything more than a foot in front of my face, and I have no doubt I'm in the one place I've been trying so hard never to return to.

I feel him.

He's watching me.

This time I'll get some answers, I need to.

"I know you're there, so you might as well show yourself."

Silence.

I sigh. The darkness around me remains silent. I ask a question, hoping this time I'll get an answer.

"How did you get here?"

In the distance, I hear a shuffle circling me.

"Like everyone else, I suppose."

I rub my eyes in annoyance before saying, "For argument's sake, let's say I don't know how that is."

Morpheus chuckles sinisterly in the darkness to my left. "You die."

The way he says those two words sends a chill over me.

"When did you die?"

"A long time ago."

"And why haven't you moved on?"

"Because I'm trapped here. I'm pretty sure we already went over that."

I try to recall my earlier dreams, and then it comes to me.

"What did you mean before?"

"When?"

"When you called me your meat suit."

Another evil laugh rings through the night around me.

"You sure you want to know?"

"Yes!"

I hear him move closer until a small ray of light from the moon casts across the left side of his face, revealing pitch-black hair and even darker eyes. "Just remember you asked."

I nod, afraid to do much else.

"Over a hundred years ago, I was trapped here. The local Djinn and Soul Eaters, as you would call them back then, cornered me after my most recent kill and they—"

"Wait. What do you mean by the most recent kill?"

He shifts in the moonlight to flash me a grin that causes me to shiver.

"What do you think I mean?"

"Just answer the question."

He rolls his eyes before submerging himself back into the darkness.

"Back in my time, it was easy to go around killing people. No one really took notice. If you knew what you were doing, you could get away with it. However, somewhere along the way, I became sloppy. I felt invincible after a kill and having done it for so long with no one catching on. I never thought they would." He remains silent for a minute until I hear him step on a branch behind me. "I killed a local teenage girl, after I had my fun with her, if you catch my drift."

My stomach does a vicious flop, almost sending me to my knees.

"Turns out, this girl was beloved by the Djinn, even though as far as I could tell, she held no magic of her own. Once I'd had my fun and ran her through with my blade, they fell upon me. I became so lost in the moment. I hadn't noticed them until it was too late."

Knowing I need to learn as much as possible, I pry further. "Then what happened?"

He re-emerges from the night. "They cornered me and pulled my soul from my body before I could blink."

I shove my hands in my pockets as I glance down at my feet. "How could they do that?"

He shrugs before turning his back to me. "It's one of their powers; I never cared to learn more about it."

"So they pulled your soul from your body, and what? Threw it here?"

"That's one way of putting it."

"What happened to your body?"

He walks out in front of me and keeps walking until he's hidden in the darkness again. "Long since decayed."

"So you intend to do what? Use my body somehow?"

"Yes. I need someone like you to be free of this place."

I decide it's best to play dumb.

"Someone like me?"

"You are a dream walker. Don't pretend with me, boy. I know you know what you are."

I swallow hard but end up choking.

"I know who you are, Will Walker."

Before I can speak, he's standing in front of me, his face mere inches from mine. "You will bring me back."

"How?"

He smiles widely before turning his back on me. "You are the one my group has been looking for. You are the ultimate dream walker. You can bring people back from the dead." He turns on me fast. "And you will bring me back, and I will take over your body as my own."

I cross my arms defiantly over my chest. Who does this guy think he is?

"And why would I do a thing like that?"

He gets in my face. "Because if you don't, then what I did to your brother will happen to everyone else in your life, except with one difference." He closes the distance between us to whisper above my ear, "this time, I'll make sure you remember every detail." He moves back from me, and the look on his face reveals just how evil this man is.

I would think he's not much older than me from the way he looks. Maybe early twenties, but the darkness that has taken hold of him has turned him into something I've never seen before. I'm terrified of who this person is and of the threats he is making. I have no doubt he will do exactly what he's threatening to do, but one thing alone moves to the front of my mind: I need to get as much information as I can in hopes he lets something slip that I can use against him, but right now, I can only think about one thing. One person.

"What do you know about what happened to West?" I demand angrily.

"Everything. After all, I was the one that killed him. Or, I should say, my followers."

A fire fills my stomach, threatening to boil over, and I have to push it back down. I need more answers, and I won't get them if I let my anger take over.

"What did you do?" I growl.

"I just told you," he says in annoyance.

I take a step closer to him, unafraid for the first time, as the rage boils in my

100

veins.

"Like you just said, I don't remember, so how about you tell me?"

He looks up at the sky with a grin before answering, "I'm afraid our time is almost up." He turns his attention back to me. "But I don't think you need me to fill in the blanks for you."

Before I can stop myself, my hands are tangled in the fabric of his shirt as I grip and yank him close. "What did you do?" I bellow in his face.

His smile grows. "Ah, so there's that backbone. Good, it came out to play because you're going to need it."

I shake him violently before getting in his face once more. "Tell me, damn it."

"Why don't you expend that energy by asking your mother the truth about you and your family."

Before I can offer my rebuttal, the darkness moves in on us as the air becomes thick.

"As I said, it appears we are out of time, little walker, until next time."

Morpheus's words wrap around me as my body becomes weightless and I'm falling.

I gasp for air as I shoot upright in my bed. Sweat drips down my face as my shirt sticks to my body.

"What the hell was that?"

Once I calm down, I turn my attention to the clock on my nightstand: 4:36 p.m. I sigh as I run my hand over my face and exit my bed. Then, removing my damp clothing from my body, I replace them with dry ones before going to the kitchen.

"There you are, sleepyhead," my mother says in her usual mellow tone.

How can she act like nothing's wrong? She was crying in her room only an hour ago. But something runs deeper here. If she really does know the truth, how could she act like everything is normal? One thing is for sure tonight, I will get some answers, but for right now, it's business as usual.

"What can I help with?"

Her smile widens on her face as she glances at me. "Could you peel and cut the potatoes for me?"

"Sure."

For the next two hours, we work together in the kitchen, prepping dinner, then sit together at a table too big for the two of us and eat in silence, like every night before. I take the dishes to the sink and begin cleaning them off.

"Will, you don't need to do that."

"I don't mind."

My mother places the last of the dishes on the counter next to the sink. "What movie will we be watching tonight?"

"I was thinking we could watch *Wanda Vision*."

"That superhero show?"

"Yeah."

She picks up the bowl that had mashed potatoes in it only minutes ago and begins to dry it with a dish towel.

"That should be interesting."

"Very," I whisper, causing her to look at me confused. "I heard it was really good."

Her smile returns as she places the bowl back in the far cabinet. "Well, everyone in this house has always liked the superhero movies, so I'm sure this will be no different."

You have no idea.

I wasn't lying when I said I've heard many good things about the show, and as my mother said, we have always watched anything with superheroes in it. However, I have another reason for my choice of TV madness. I think this show will line up with the talk we need to have perfectly. After all, Wanda is so messed up from the life she's been dealt that she creates a new world of her own. Kind of like I can with my power. It's different, but I can see some similarities between Wanda and me. She lost the love of her life and her brother, while I lost my brother and my father, so I think we can relate.

"I'll finish up here, honey. Why don't you go get it ready on the TV?"

"Sounds good."

I exit the kitchen, turning to glance at my mother. The mother I've always known was taken from me when I learned who I really am. Our relationship is now tainted with these secrets she has kept from me all my life.

After sitting alone in the dark and seeing the evil that lurks there, I have no doubt she did it to protect me, but it doesn't change the lies, the secrets, and now the danger we are in. It also didn't protect West from Morpheus. Maybe if we had known the truth, things would have been different.

At the thought of this secret having cost me our family, the anger rears its ugly head once more, and it takes everything in me to beat it back. I know I have the right to be angry, but my mother would never purposely do anything to hurt my brother or me. She's always done everything she can to protect us and keep us happy.

I sigh as the picture of *Wanda Vision* takes over the TV screen. Wanda has always been an interesting character to me. She's so strong, and the things she is capable of are insane. I know Sage, and even Morpheus have said I'm the ultimate dream walker, but the thought of having all this power and not knowing what I'm really capable of scares me. I've only scratched the surface of my gift, and I'm afraid to see what someone like Morpheus could do with this power. He was already a killer, and if he ever returned, I know he would be again. But with this power, he could turn into some *Freddy Kruger* wannabe. Then no one would be safe.

"You look far away. Is everything OK?" My mother's voice pulls me from my fear.

I turn around to see her carrying two bowls of popcorn, offering me one before she takes a seat on the couch.

"Sorry, I was thinking."

I sit next to her with my popcorn.

"Want to talk about it?" She asks, concern in her voice.

"Yes, more than anything. But maybe we could watch a few episodes first."

Confusion fills her features as I turn on the show. She looks at me for a few more moments before turning her attention to the screen in front of us. We get lost in the story for a few hours before my mother speaks.

"OK, Will. That was three shows. Now tell me what's going on."

I sigh, unable to look at her. "I don't know where to start."

"Just say whatever comes to your mind."

I close my eyes. "Why didn't you tell me I wasn't normal?"

I hear her suck in a long deep breath, causing me to open my eyes and look at her.

"What…"

The rest of the words get trapped in her throat as she stares at me.

"I know, Mom."

Fear is embedded in all of her features. "What do you know?"

"I would say, 'why don't you tell me what you think I know,' but for some reason, I think you've kept more secrets from me than I know."

"It's not like that."

"How isn't it? You lied to me for almost eighteen years. My whole life has been a lie, and now West is dead because of it."

My mother looks like I slapped her in the face as she says, "What are you talking about?"

"He told me."

"Who told you? What did they say?"

My hands turn to fists at my sides. "The man in my dreams. He told me he killed West. He said he killed him because of what I am and what I can do."

She places a hand just above my wrist. "Baby, you were only dreaming. What happened to West wasn't your fault, do you hear me?"

"No. It was yours. You kept this from me. From us. And it cost us everything."

My words make my mother cringe as I see tears forming in her eyes.

"Will, West made his choice, and I know he would do it again."

"What are you talking about?"

Her hand squeezes me lightly. "He protected you."

"So it was my fault?"

She shakes her head. "No, no, none of this was your fault, Will."

"What haven't you told me?"

She looks away before answering, "There is a lot. Too much to tell you in one night, I'm afraid."

"Well, start somewhere."

She takes in a deep breath before continuing, "I guess the best place to start is at the beginning." She settles back into her seat as she sighs. "Your father works for this place called the Company. They look for people with gifts, people like you and your brother. By now, I'm guessing you know you are what they call a dream walker."

I nod.

"Do you know what your powers are?"

"Mostly."

"And do you know you are the only walker of your kind?"

I nod.

"The Company would use this program to show what men and women had the gene lying dormant in them. They would then seek them out and drug them. They did this in hopes of reawakening the walker gene that had been suppressed many years ago. Once this was done, they would match up couples based on statistics of who could produce a child with the gift. Many did, but over the last hundred years, none had the power they needed."

"But I do."

"Your brother was a walker, as well, but he didn't have the power I knew you did. You never showed any real sign of your gift, but I knew."

"How?"

She smiles lightly. "Call it mother's intuition."

"So you and Dad work for this place. For the Company."

"Your father does, yes."

"Is that why he left?"

She nods.

"So he was, what, planted into your life?"

"That's one way of putting it. Once your father was recruited, they learned I was a possible carrier of the gene, and they told your father to find a way into my life, so he did. We became close, and he was drugging my fluids with the formula to reawaken the gene."

"Why did you stay with him?"

"To this day, your father doesn't know I know about his part in everything, and he doesn't know about you. Your brother and I talked many years ago. I told him what he was, what you were, and that we needed to keep it a secret from you and your father. I knew it was the only way to keep you safe."

"But why not tell me?"

"Because the moment you knew and used your powers, the Company could find you. Track you."

"Like Sage said," I whisper.

Her eyes turn to slits as recognition of something shines in them, something not good from the look of things.

"Sage? What does she have to do with anything?"

"She's a walker. It's because of her I know what I am. She's been teaching me."

My mother becomes uneasy in her seat. "Will, what do you know about this girl?"

"Why?"

"Remember how I told you the Company works. They put your father into my life. They do that all the time to gain something they want. Maybe it wasn't an accident, you two meeting. I'm not saying she works for them, but maybe they let her escape. Maybe they planted it in her head where to go."

"You think they would go through all of that, and she wouldn't know about it?"

"The company has a way of getting in your head. She wouldn't even know they did it. Your father talked with someone years ago, and I heard them mention Morpheus. They said he was trapped somewhere in the dream world, and only the ultimate dream walker could get him out. They said the walker would bring Morpheus back to life, and he would take over the walker's body. He can only survive here in the body of a walker. Any walker, from what I heard, but his soul would eat away at the body unless it were someone like you." She leans in close to me. "This place only cares about the end goal, and that's to bring him back. They will do anything to make it happen. Even mind warp a young girl like Sage."

"Then where do I go from here?"

"Just be careful. Maybe see if she's willing to let you dream walk into her mind. Sometimes you can see memories, which might allow you to see what happened to her while she was there. You'll both be better off knowing."

I nod in agreement, but something is still eating at me.

"You and West knew what I was all this time. You're saying Dad didn't, but how can you be so sure?"

"I don't think he would have left here without you if he knew."

"So he left us to return to the Company?"

She nods. "Your father believed West was the one they wanted, and when he died, he returned to the base to try again."

"He just up and left his family for another one?"

"I don't know for sure. I haven't spoken to him since he left. All I know is your father and I kept a lot of secrets from each other."

"And from me."

"Yes, and I'm sorry I lied, but I wanted you to have a normal childhood, and I wanted you to be safe for as long as possible."

"I appreciate what you were trying to do, but now we are all in danger. He's coming for me, Mom, and unless I give him what he wants, he will kill everyone."

She squeezes my hand. "Remember when I said your father and I kept secrets from each other?"

I nod.

"My family started a school a few generations back. When I learned who you would become, I became involved in it again, but at a distance, so your father wouldn't know."

"A school? For what?"

"For people like you. It's warded, so no one can see it other than who we allow. So you have to be going to the school, or be accepted into the fold, to know where it is or how to enter."

"OK. And?"

"Now that you know the truth, I want to take you there."

I stand, peering down at her in astonishment. "You want me to just leave?"

"You're not safe here."

"You think?" I shout as I begin pacing the living room. "But taking me away isn't going to change anything. It's only going to piss this guy off."

"You are what's important, Will. If they find you—"

"Don't you think I know? I know someone like him could be dangerous if he takes over my body. He's a killer, and with me as his host, no one would be safe, but running isn't the answer."

She stands, striding to my side before taking my hands, making me stop.

"OK, Will. I'll do whatever you want, but we have a lot to talk about, and you have a lot you need to learn if we are going to do this your way. I don't want the school taken off the table."

"I can live with that. I need a drink. You want anything?" I ask as I walk to the kitchen.

"Water, please," she says as she sits back on the couch.

As I pour our water, I think about how messed up my life is now. How naive and in the dark I was to believe that my brother's death and my father leaving was the worst thing that could happen.

Boy, was I wrong.

Chapter 13

My mother and I talked about dad and West for the next hour. She told me she didn't think her husband would come back, and though she missed him, she loved me more and wanted to keep as much distance between us as possible. She told me everything she knew about the Company and Morpheus, which was pretty much everything I already knew.

She told me how West would go into my mind and place barriers to keep my dreams hidden from the Company and our father. He couldn't morph or change them or take away the nightmares I would have, but he protected me in every way an older brother could. My mother told me West was one of the strongest walkers they had seen, and he had powers that no other walkers before him did, like the protective barriers. West was how the Company knew my mother and father were a strong match and that they were on the right track with the walker matches they were making.

Now the change in my dreams finally makes sense. Why they have become darker and more frequent after my brother died, and who Morpheus finally made his way into them. With my brother gone the protection I never knew I had was now gone as well.

It was almost ten at night when we decided to table the conversation for tomorrow. My mother was adamant about me considering attending the school her family ran. After all, I would apparently be taking it over one day. So I told her we would talk about it more another day.

As I head to my bedroom, sleep threatens to swallow me up before I reach my door. Even though I had that cat nap earlier, I'm still dead on my feet. Maybe it's the mental exhaustion winning. My dreams have become lucid, so even when I'm sleeping, I feel awake, so when I get up, I'm as tired as I was when I laid down.

My feet glide along the floor, and I barely see my bed through my blurry eyes as I trip and fall onto it in a heap. Within seconds, sleep is rising to meet me.

* * *

"So, what did we learn?" Morpheus's voice finds me in the darkness.

I remain silent.

"What happened to that fire you had on your last visit?"

No response.

"Come on, Will. I know you can do better than the silent treatment."

Nope.

"Fine, I'll go first." He moves in behind me as he whispers in my ear. "Did Sage find you yet?"

My heart beats wildly in my chest, but I remain silent. Could my mother have been right?

"Your silence tells me she has." He backs away, circling me once more. "Tell me, has dear Will fallen for the fiery girl? What story did she feed you about her family?"

My voice is lost in my chest.

"Let me guess. She said her family wanted nothing to do with her or the better one. Her family left or died." He looks over at me as he stops. "Am I close?"

He's lying. Sage, of course, he would know about her. He did take her prisoner.

"Don't worry. I get it. You don't want to think someone you want to bed could betray you. I've been there. The betrayal stings like a bitch, but I promise it only lasts a moment."

"You're lying," I mumble.

"Oh, dear me, no. I wish I were, but everything I have ever said to you has been the truth. Just like when I say," he leans in close to me before saying his next words, *"killing her, seeing the light leave her eyes, will bring you pleasure like you've never imagined."*

I push him away from me, hard. "I'm not like you."

His smile grows until it takes up his whole face. "Maybe not yet. But you will be."

I shake my head. "It will never happen."

He starts to circle me. "You may not think so, but I've seen it. You will release me. It has been foretold."

"I will never let you out of this cage, this is where you belong."

"Maybe so, and I'm sure you believe it, but trust me when I tell you, you will free me from this place, and it will be very soon. I want you to know that when you do," suddenly he disappears from my sight, and then his following words come from behind me, sending a chill running through my soul, *"I will take pleasure in making you watch me kill everyone you love before taking your body as my own."*

I turn around to find nothing but darkness.

"One last thing. Have you noticed the uncontrollable urge to take her to bed yet?"

I say nothing.

"Your silence speaks volumes, my boy. A little word of advice. Don't fight it." He sneers, *"the longer you do, the more painful it will become. You'll learn shortly what I mean by that. It's a neat trick, you see. Knowing who your parents are and their biology allowed me to develop the perfect...poison, I suppose you should call it. It pulls you both to each other until you give in and then. Well, then the real fun begins."*

A million questions are running wild in my mind, but I can't get one out. Not one. This guy is completely insane. How can you mess with people's lives like this and not feel something?

"Tick tock William, Tick tock."

"Will, wake up."

* * *

My mother's voice calls to me somewhere in the distance. Her hands cover me in the familiar warmth and comfort, grounding my mind and centering me. I peel my eyes apart as they take in my mother's fear-stricken expression. I sit up slowly, careful not to hit her forehead with my own as she moves back on the bed.

"You were yelling."

I turn to her in surprise. "I was?"

She nods.

"What was I saying?"

"You kept repeating Sage's name."

My heart thumps away loudly in my chest at the sound of her name. I move away from my mother and off the bed. I go to my dresser and unplug my Galaxy from its charger, seeing it's at full percentage. I barely open the contacts before my mother reaches my side.

"What is it?"

I pull up Sage's number and hit the text icon. "I saw him again."

"Him? Him who?"

"Morpheus."

The air around us changes at the mention of his name.

"What did he say?"

The text screen pops up, and I type away.

Can you stop by??? It's important.

I lock my screen and turn my attention back to my mother. "He made a comment."

"About Sage?"

I nod.

"What did he say?"

I walk over to my bed and mindlessly begin fixing the sheets. "He, in his own way, confirmed what you thought they did to her."

She steps towards me as my eyes shift to her movement, causing her to stop.

"We need to warn her. If they implanted things in her mind to get her here, they might still be able to get to her in her dream state, and if they do that-"

"Then the Company will know where to find me."

My mother nods and her worry becomes clear in her body language and all I want to do is promise her nothing will happen and that we will both be OK, but I know I can't promise that. One thing we always promised each other was never to lie, no matter what.

I straighten up, turning back towards her. "Morpheus may know my name, but I think if he knew who I was, they would have shown up here by now. I only hope that what they did to Sage was only something to get her to find me."

"I do too, but if they did that, then you can be sure they are tracking her, and if they are, they know where she is. They may not know you're a walker or the one they are looking for yet, but they will soon enough. We need to know what happened to her when she was there. It's the only way to protect you both."

"Already on it," I say as I pull open my door, making my way to the kitchen.

I hear my mother's light footsteps as she follows behind me. More than anything, I hope she's right, and this is just a ruse to create a rift between me and those I'm closest to. A way to seclude me and make me weak so he could find his in. But for some reason, I can't shake this feeling deep in my gut as I replay our time together in the dream world I built. How distant she was and unwilling to talk to me or shed light on the sudden change in her behavior towards me.

Could Morpheus be telling me the truth?

Is Sage working for them?

I know I need to ask her, but there's no going back once I do. I may not know her all that well, but I know her well enough to tell if she's lying or holding something back from me. I feel my phone vibrate in my pocket, and I quickly pull it out to see Sage's reply.

On my way.

Time to face the music.

Chapter 14

"Where's the fire?" Sage says as she makes her way up the walkway in haste.

"We need to talk."

"I gathered that much from the text." Her eyes lock with mine before she continues, "What's going on?"

"I need to ask you something, and I need you not to lie to me."

I move to the patio chair and take a seat, Sage follows my lead.

"OK. What is it?"

My heart beats wildly in my chest as my mouth suddenly turns dry.

"I saw Morpheus again."

"When?"

"Tonight."

She moves slightly in her seat. "And?"

"He said something."

She sighs, and I can hear the annoyance in her action.

"Out with it, Will. What did he say?"

"He told me you aren't who you claim to be."

She remains quiet.

"Is there something I should know?"

More silence. Fear takes hold at the thought that this is deeper than we thought. Maybe she is working for them.

"Sage." She turns her attention back in my direction, "are you working for the Company?"

"Will." Thea's voice takes me by surprise as I turn my head in the direction it came from to see her walking up the cement.

I stand, turning to Sage, "Wait here."

I reach Thea in a few short strides. "Hey, what's up?"

She looks around me to see Sage sitting in the chair on my step. "Am I interrupting something?"

I glance back at Sage, "No."

"I didn't think you would have company this early in the morning." Thea pauses as I turn back to her, "Did she stay the night?" Her last words come out in a choking noise.

"Are you OK?"

"Yes. Sorry. I just. What is she doing here so early, Will?"

From the tone of her voice, I know something isn't right. Thea has never cared about other girls being around or even focused much on things happening in my life, for that matter. So, why does she seem so on edge with the fact that Sage is here right now? Why would she care if she spent the night?

"No, Thea. She didn't stay the night. I texted her because I left my book at her house the other day, and I needed it for school later."

"So she came over at six in the morning to drop off a book." She states before folding her arms over her chest.

I know she doesn't believe me, but I don't have the time to worry about her feelings or why she is acting the way she is right now. I need to figure out if I can trust Sage, and that's the only thing I can focus on right now.

"Thea, why are you here so early? School will be starting soon."

Her cheeks turn a deep shade of pink as she turns her attention towards her feet. "I texted you, and when I was driving by, I saw you out here, so I stopped."

"But was there a reason you stopped? And where were you going this early in the morning?"

Curiosity runs through every cell of my being as Thea glances back at Sage once more. "I wanted to see if you wanted to carpool to school today. Was hoping maybe you, me, and Trey could do something later after school."

"I would like that." I throw a thumb over my shoulder in Sage's direction, "I just have to handle a few more things here first. Want to meet me back here at 7:40 a.m. and head to school together?"

She nods in agreement.

"Great. I'll see you in an hour."

I start to turn back to Sage, but Thea grabs my wrist, pulling my attention back to her.

"Will."

"Yeah."

"Be careful with her, OK?"

I hear the worry in her voice, and I wonder if maybe she senses something about Sage that I haven't for some reason.

"I will," I mumble with a smile.

Thea removes her hand from my body as she smiles and turns away from me. Confusion fills my mind as I think about what the hell just happened. Thea has never been known to be the jealous kind, and even if she were, she would never be that way with me. We've never been more than friends. If anything, she might see me as a brother. In the fifteen years we've known each other, Thea has never once looked in my direction with any interest that would surpass that of a friend. Even though for many years, I wished she would.

"Everything OK?" Sage asks from my side.

I turn my attention back to her, "Yeah, fine."

"That conversation seemed a little tense."

"It was nothing. But I need you to answer my question, Sage."

"I think we should go inside first."

I'm about to protest, but then I remember how she told me before that it's not safe out here, that someone could be watching. We may have ourselves cloaked, but being inside my home is safer since we put up the extra protection. I nod as I make my way back towards my front door.

Once we enter, I close the door quickly behind me, ready to get this over with.

"Well?"

"I need you to understand something, Will. What I told you before was all the truth. But I left some things out."

"Like what?"

She turns her back to me as she becomes uneasy, pacing my living room. "I didn't escape the Company as I said. They let me go."

"Why?"

Fear fills my chest, causing it to tighten.

"The people who run the Company have a way to keep in contact with Morpheus. Even though they aren't walkers themselves, they have ways to enter the dream world. That's how they found you, and that's how he tells them what he wants them to do."

She falls quiet for a moment, and just as I'm about to push her for more information, she faces me with tears in her eyes.

"They took my family and told me I needed to find you and get close to you. They told me I was to check in once I did, and they would come and get you."

Morpheus was right when he said that betrayal can be crippling as her words turn my legs to mush, and I lean on the wall closest to me for support.

"I need you to know, Will, I didn't betray you." She cries.

"You just said-"

"I said they told me what to do, but once I met you, I couldn't do it. I couldn't turn you over to them. I started to feel something for you, Will. Something deeper than-"

"Save me your lies. I don't want to hear them."

I head for the kitchen with Sage following on my heels, my legs giving out underneath me every few steps.

"Will, please, you need to hear me. I didn't give them any information on you, I swear. I couldn't. I tried to keep you at a distance, to be mean, but that didn't work. Then, I tried to seduce you to throw you off my track, but you surprised me when you turned me down. Everything I tried to keep you at arm's length turned against me. Your actions only pulled me closer to you. I needed to hand you over, don't you understand? They have my family but once I really got to know you I knew no matter how hard I would try to convince myself to turn you in that it wouldn't work. You may be our only chance at surviving all of this. I can't put myself and my family above every other walker out there and I can't….I can't lose you too."

I place my hands on the counter, looking in her direction. "How can I believe a word you're saying?"

She places her hand over mine. I look down at them before pulling mine out from under her's as a sob sounds in her throat at my reaction.

"Will, I didn't tell them anything. I swear I didn't. This whole time I've been trying to teach you how to protect yourself from them. I never reported back. They have my family, Will and I still told them nothing."

"Why?"

"Why, what?" She chokes out the words.

"Why are you teaching me how to use my power?"

"Because you need to learn, and I know more than you do. I couldn't just sit back and watch something happen to you, not if I could help it. I would feel responsible for not training you and teaching you what I know if something happened."

"Why didn't you turn me in?"

She rubs at her arm feverishly, breaking eye contact. "I couldn't."

"But, why?"

"For two reasons. One is if anyone can put an end to them, it's you. If me, my family, and all the other families out there have a chance at being free, at living a normal life, then we need you on our side, not taken over by some crazy psycho. We are in danger now, but could you imagine if he was free running around? Nowhere would be safe, and no protection spells, wards, or spice concoctions I used would matter."

"And the other reason?"

Her cheeks turn red before she turns her back on me, walking back toward the front door. I move in front of her blocking her path to the door.

"The other reason, Sage?"

She lifts her eyes slowly until they find mine. "I think you already know the other reason."

"I need you to say it."

118

Sage closes her eyes before turning away from me. I catch her cheeks flush before I'm looking at her backside. She remains quiet for a moment before she chokes out her next words, so distorted, I'm not sure I'm hearing them correctly.

"Will, I think…I think I'm falling in love with you."

Her words ignite something deep inside, and I lose all control over my body and senses. I try to focus on what Morpheus said about what they did to us, telling myself that this isn't real. What we are both feeling isn't natural, but it makes no difference. I can't stop myself, and before I know it, my hands are on her waist, turning her around to face me. Seeing the tears running down her face, I absently wipe them away before cupping her cheek in my hand and pulling her lips to mine.

This time she doesn't stop me, doesn't turn away, but instead, falls into the embrace as she wraps her arms around my neck, holding onto me for dear life. My mind is screaming at me to stop, telling me this isn't right and most certainly not the time, but my body doesn't listen. It's taken on a life of its own as my hands roam and explore her body, as our lips collide with one another in a hot wet mess.

My hand travels up the back of her cotton shirt, releasing a moan from her lips, causing mine to vibrate from the intensity. My hands are firm on her hot skin as I press her to my body and the world around us disappears. My body feels heavy as my breath becomes stuck in my throat. My head is spinning as everything around us becomes silent. The only noise is our panting.

I fight to take back control of my actions.

Clawing away at the force now surrounding me.

Trapped.

Silent.

I focus until I feel the snap, and suddenly I'm back in control. Feeling her soft, moist lips against mine as our tongues danced together in perfect unison. Nothing has ever felt so right and yet so wrong simultaneously. I groan against her embrace, not wanting to end it but knowing I need to.

My hands grip her skin as they become firm on her hips, moving her back slowly. Once our lips separate, we both gasp for breath like we've been underwater for too long. I pull back a few inches as my vision becomes less blurry. I look beyond Sage to find my living room gone, and in its place are lots of different trees.

I move further away from her as I remove my hands from her body and do a 360 turn. There are trees for as far as I can see, and deep in the distance, I can just make out a body of water. My heart contracts as I take the cool mid morning air into my lungs. I feel them expanding as the realization hits me.

"Oh. My. God."

Sage moves next to me, taking in our surroundings. "Where are we?"

"I think we are in my dreamscape."

Her eyes widen as her attention returns to me. "What? How?"

"I don't know. You're the dream walker thesaurus not me. How could this even happen? We were both awake." I turn my attention back to the view around us, "Weren't we?"

"Yes." She says with complete certainty, "I know for sure we were. I've learned to look for the differences. It can get confusing at times but the more you practice, the easier you can see the differences between the real world and your dreams."

"So the question remains." I turn back to her, "If you're certain we were both awake, then how did we end up here?"

Sage shrugs her shoulders, "I honestly have no idea. I've never heard of this happening. For all I know, it shouldn't be possible."

I gesture to the scenery around us with my hands. "Looks like it's possible to me."

She takes a step back, putting her hands up in surrender. "Don't shoot the messenger. If I knew this was possible, I would have been teaching you how to do it. Something like this could come in handy. I knew the ultimate dream walker could bring people here, but not like this, you had to be asleep and as far as I know they had to too. You being awake and pulling us here opens many doors. If we were under random attack you could pull everyone in here at that moment."

I look at her in confusion, and it only takes her a moment to realize where she lost me.

"What I mean is, if you brought our whole bodies here and not just our subconscious and the Company can't enter this world, then you can bring everyone here to keep them safe until we figure out how to bring the Company to its knees and like I mentioned being able to do this in your awakened state will make it a lot easier to keep everyone safe."

Her words send my mind spinning. This could be the answer we've been searching for, a way to protect everyone from Morpheus and his men, at least for the time being. I know I can't give him what he wants, but I also refuse to lose anyone else I care about. I look over at Sage as something dawns on me. The pull, the connection I felt to her before this happened. The total loss and control of myself. Something in that moment allowed me to bring us here. Now, I just need to figure out how to trigger that again. This time, without kissing her.

"How do we know our bodies aren't unconscious on my living room floor right now?" I ask.

"We don't. But your Mom's home right now, right?"

I nod.

"Well, let's take our time here and then figure out how to get back and when we do, we can ask her if she went into the living room at all while we were here. If she says yes, we can ask if she saw our bodies. Although, I'm sure if she did, she would try to wake us up," she chuckles. "Right now, we should focus on how you got us here."

I feel the heat rise to my cheeks at her statement. It's not something I want to talk about, but I know if we are going to figure this out, us being uncomfortable has to take a back seat.

"Well, we were kissing."

She smiles, "I know that. But what were you feeling, thinking?"

I take a step away from her as I rub the back of my neck, "I was thinking about how I shouldn't be kissing you."

"Oh."

"My mind was saying one thing while my body was acting on its own."

She moves next to me, and I fear the following words coming out of her

121

mouth.

"OK. So, your body reacted without your mind telling it to." Her eyebrows meet as she looks into the distance. "Can you tell me what emotions you felt?"

"Frustration. Annoyed and," I look at her as the pain becomes apparent in her features as I recall what Morpheus told me about us, but I decide now isn't the time to tell her. "I felt like I didn't want to stop kissing you, but I told myself I needed to."

Her eyes connect with mine. "OK. Maybe if you focus on those emotions again, it might work. Was there anything else you remember?"

"I was really dizzy. I couldn't make out anything around me other than us."

She nods. "OK. That's easy. So, when you try this again, I think if you focus hard enough on the person with you and the feelings you are having, it should be enough to pull them through the world with you."

"Sage?"

"Yes."

I know she might not have the answer to this question, and I don't know if I'm more afraid that she won't or that she will, but I know I need to ask it.

"If I can do this, something you didn't even know about, what else do you think I can do?"

She shrugs lightly at my side before speaking. "I once heard that the ultimate dream walker could take his powers into the real world, that he could transform things there as well as here. Some even said he could control the elements and make light in the dark. But again, those things we never confirmed, so no one paid them much mind." She turns her attention back to the body of water in front of us. "But one thing I know for sure. If you can do this, you can definitely bring someone back from the dead."

West.

"How would that even work?"

She looks at me with fear in her eyes. "Will, that isn't something you should think about. People don't talk about the cost, but I'm sure there is one to something like that, and it won't be something small."

"That's not what I asked."

She closes her eyes, looks away from me, and releases a sigh. "From what I've heard, you have to be here, in the dreamscape. If the person wants to be found, they will make themselves known in some way."

"Like how?"

"Sometimes it's a whisper, someone calling to you. Other times you'll see them. Then, it's up to you to search this world and find them. Once you do, it's like everything else. You hold onto them and focus on them as you wake yourself up. Once you do, they should have come back to the real world with you."

"Alive?"

She nods.

I look deep into the forest and remember a few days ago when I woke in a sweat after hearing West calling for me.

"I know what you're thinking, Will and I get it, but I need to warn you. You do this, and the consequences might not be something you can take back."

I turn to her as hope fills my body. "He's my brother, Sage. I can't do this without him and learning that Morpheus is responsible for his death and he's gone because of me, I have to do everything I can to bring him back. I can't remember what happened that day. All I know is what people have told me."

She places her hand on my shoulder. "What have they told you?"

I look at her hand on me and then into her eyes as the pain makes its way to the surface. "They told me he died saving me."

I turn away from her, not wanting to see the look in her eyes.

"Will, I don't know what happened, and I didn't know your brother, but if that's true, then you would be dishonoring him by doing what you're thinking. He saved you. He had an honorable death, one that most of us say we would do for someone we love but never have to. He did, and he made his choice."

I move away from her. "You're right. He did, and now I'm making mine."

I hear the defeat in her voice, "I can't talk you out of this, can I?"

I shake my head.

I feel her place her hand in mine. "If this is something you need to do,

I understand, and I'll be here to help in any way I can. I just want you to promise me one thing."

I glance down at her. "And what's that?"

"Think about the cost, what it could be if you do this, and if you'll be able to live with it. Think about it for a few days before you try it. He will still be there waiting."

I nod. She isn't asking for much, and she's right; I should think about it. This isn't something small, and if everyone could do it, no one would die. Maybe I'm being selfish or want to right something I wronged. Because of me, my family split, and my brother lost his life. The least I can do is find the answers and bring him back.

"Maybe we should try to head back now; see about those other powers you mentioned. It's better to know and see what my strengths are so I can get them under control."

Sage smiles up at me before squeezing my hand lightly.

"Maybe. Maybe I should hold you." I mumble.

She moves in closer to me until my arms are wrapped around her, my heart beating a little louder as my mind runs away with me. Maybe once this is all over, we could be happy together despite whatever the Company did to us. I know we feel a connection, but something inside tells me this isn't the path I'm meant to follow. Thinking about it causes my vision to blur as the thought of hurting her crosses my mind.

No matter who she is and why she came here, I don't want to hurt her. If what I saw in her eyes and what she said to me was true, I know she wants what my body is telling me I want, too. I need to tread lightly here, or we are both going to get burned. Even though my mind is telling my body not to push this with her, my hands move her closer to me as my heart beats in my chest and the urge to kiss her and never stop enters my mind.

Before I try to silence the thoughts, the world around us disappears, and my body turns heavy as the world falls away.

Chapter 15

"Mom!" I yell into the dark as I take in my new surroundings. We're back in my home.

"Mom!"

I release Sage and head towards the hall as my mother emerges from her room.

"Will? What's wrong?" She asks with fear in her eyes.

I pull her into a strong hug as she does the same.

I move back, looking down at her, "Have you been in the living room lately?"

She looks at me, confused. "I went to the kitchen a little while ago to get something for lunch. I looked for you but didn't see you, so I figured maybe you and Sage went to school."

"Right, school. So, you didn't see us in the living room?"

Her expression turns to concern. "There was no one in there, Will. I looked. What's going on?"

At a loss for words, Sage moves closer and says, "Will just did something that shouldn't be possible and something that could give us more time to figure out how to stop the Company."

My mother looks from Sage to me. "What's she talking about, Will?"

"Somehow, I brought us both into my dreamscape, but this time it wasn't just our minds. It was our whole body."

My mother and I separate.

"How is that possible?"

"I don't know, but I did it."

Sage, looking uncomfortable, says, "I've heard that the ultimate walker had powers different from the others, but some people said they can do what Will just did." She looks at me, "That, and a lot more."

My mother turns her attention back towards Sage. "What do you know about what the Company did to the walker community? What changes have there been to the children in your generation?"

My mother's intense gaze causes Sage to take a step back.

"I know that Will is the only one of his power level. There are a lot of walkers who can change their dreams and even enter others. However, I've met a few who can do more than that and heard rumors that some of us can grow into something stronger." She looks at me, "I was told I was one of those who would be able to manipulate the real world eventually, but I've never been able to."

My mother's eyes widen but I see in them something like understanding. "Manipulate the real world. What does that even mean?"

Sage looks at my mother, and I can see how nervous she is. I've never known my mother to make anyone other than her kids nervous.

"We can change things. For example, your front door. We could make it disappear and make a door appear somewhere else. Things like that."

"How many of you are there that can do that?"

"I don't know. It was only talked about, but I never really saw anyone do it before, so it could have been only talk."

My mother shakes her head before turning away, "No. I don't think it was."

She disappears into the hallway, leaving Sage and me to look at each other in confusion. I take my first step to follow after her leaving Sage to take up the rear. I find my mother on her bed surrounded by paperwork.

"Mom, what is all this?" I bend over and pick up a page.

Date: 05/20/1984
   Test #803

We injected the subject with serum #598 today. No changes.

Date: 06/04/1984

Still no change in subject. However, we have learned she is with child and will monitor closely.

Date: 01/11/1985

The subject gave birth today. Running tests on subjects A and B. Subject B showed no signs of walker gene. Being only a few hours old, maybe it's too soon to tell. I will continue monitoring.

Date: 10/10/1990

Subject B's tests for the gene have come back positive. Now it's simply a waiting game. I will continue to monitor closely.

Date: 01/11/1996

Subject B turned eleven today, and the walker genes appear stronger in her than in the past subjects. I see great promise.

Date: 06/04/1996

Subject B escaped today. We must find her. She may hold the key to what we have been working towards.

I read over the dates carefully a few more times. I can't be reading this right. I look up at my mother, who is still running her hands over the mess on her bed.

"Mom."

Nothing.

I flash the paper in front of her. "Mom, what is this?"

Pulled from her trance, she glances at me as her eyes turn dark. Sage moves next to me, taking the paper lightly from my hand and giving it a once over.

"I know what this is."

I pull my attention away from my mother for a second.

"It's from the Company." She glances up at me, "Remember how I told you they did the experiments?"

I nod.

"Well, this is one of them."

My mind explodes in my head as I turn to my mother. "Tell me what I'm thinking is wrong."

Her eyes find mine, and the horror and sadness in them are apparent.

"Mom," I say in a soothing tone as I bend over and take her in my arms.

We sit there for a moment as she sobs lightly into my shoulder, her body shaking mine slightly. After a few minutes, she calms down, pulling back from me and wiping her cheeks.

"We haven't had much time to talk about what I know about the Company and why." My mother mumbles.

I take the page from Sage and place it on the bed in front of my mother.

"So, what I'm thinking is right?"

Sage moves closer, "What?"

My mother nods. "Yes. Subject A was my mother, and I was subject B. We were part of the gene program at the Company."

Sage's eyes go wide. "Wow! Mind blown. You mean you were there?"

My mother nods. "Yes, for almost twelve years."

"How did you escape?" Sage asks the question before I can.

"My mother, she sacrificed herself so that I could get out."

The pain on my mother's face awakens new anger deep in my soul.

"How did you survive? You were so young."

She turns her attention back to the mess of paperwork on her bed, clearly still looking for something.

"I was lucky. We had friends my mother had kept in touch with; other walkers who got away. Don't ask me how she did it because I don't know. But, they stayed off the Company's radar, so she sent me there. I was safe for many years, and they taught me a lot. But once they died, I was on my own, and soon after, your father found me. I didn't know until I was pregnant with West who your father was. By then, it was too late to leave, and I knew the best thing I could do was stay in touch with the school in secret. My mother's parents kept it going, hoping she would get out one day. The family I stayed with reconnected me with my grandparents, and that's how I learned about the school."

"Why didn't you go there? To the school."

"I was held captive in one place for my childhood years, and I didn't want that for my adult life, but when I had your brother, I knew I had to keep the lines of communication open just in case I had to send him there for his own protection. I didn't like the thought, but I would rather him end up in some place where he's free and safe over that place."

"You came in here when we talked about other walkers having the power of morphing the real world into what they wanted. Why?"

Her attention falls solely back on the bed. "There were tests they ran while I was there, and I have the paperwork somewhere. I remember at a young age doing something like Sage suggested, but because the family I stayed with and the school didn't know these powers were possible, and I couldn't remember doing it, they never tried to train us on it. But once Sage said it, the memory returned, and I knew I could do what she mentioned. I wanted to find the paperwork in hopes that there was a list of the people who could do it and see if any escaped, so, maybe we can find them. The more firepower we have against the Company, the better."

"That's a really good idea," Sage says before taking a spot on the bed to look through the mess.

My mind is swimming. I don't hear another word they share. Anger bubbles inside, fighting to break free. This has to stop; these people are messing with people's lives. Growing up in that prison is no life. My mother lost her childhood and my grandmother because of these monsters. I'll be damned if anyone else does.

"Hey, Will, when were Thea and Trey born?" My mother asks.

I move over to the bed, looking down at the paper in her hands seeing the date reads:

Date: 12/08/2004

Subject C on gene testing gave birth to twins today, a boy and a girl. Only a few hours old and already testing positive for the walker gene. This could mean our experiments on their parents have worked to amplify their offspring's walker gene and, along with it, their powers. Morpheus will be happy with the findings.

The room spins around me as I stumble backward. I hear my mother and Sage's worried cries, but I can't focus on anything. Thea and Trey fill my mind as fear for them seeps into my bones. I feel the earth pulling me down, and soon I'm on my knees. I feel hands on my body, but I can't focus.

"Thea. Trey." I whisper their names.

I feel the ground under me shake, but I know I'm only imagining it as the room is spinning. I hear my mother and Sage gasp as their hands leave my body, and the world begins to calm.

"How did we get here?"

The sound of Thea's voice causes my head to jerk up. I blink a few times, not able to believe what I'm seeing. I have to be hallucinating.

"Mrs. Walker?" Thea's voice fills the room.

I stand slowly, taking in the people in the room one at a time. My mother, amazement all over her face. Sage looks horrified, and Trey and Thea look unsure, like I am, that they are here.

I close the distance between us until I'm standing right in front of Thea. I reach out and take her hand in mine.

"You're really here."

"Will, what's going on? One second we are in school, and the next, I'm here. I waited for you and called this morning, but you never answered." Thea's voice cracks.

My mother moves in next to us as she looks in my direction. "That's a good question."

I glance at my mother. "I don't know. I saw the paper, and then I got overwhelmed like earlier, before Sage and I ended up in my dreamscape, and

I could only think about Thea and Trey," I look back at them, "and now here they are."

Sage's voice is so low I barely hear her. "I've never heard of anything like this."

Thea grabs my arm, pulling my attention back to her. "Will. What's going on? How did we get here?"

My eyes lock with her's as fear pounds away inside my chest. "We have a lot to talk about."

Chapter 16

"I had my suspicions, but I didn't want to say anything in case I was wrong," Thea says as she moves uneasily in her seat next to me on the couch. "Could you imagine telling someone you've known your whole life that you can walk into people's dreams?" She smiles as our eyes meet, "I guess you could." She looks over to Sage, "and you're a walker as well?"

Sage nods.

I place my hand on Thea's to pull her attention back to me. Once she looks back in my direction, I remove my limb from her.

"She escaped from the Company."

"Well, actually-"

Sage begins before I cut her off with a stern look, hoping she understands.

I turn back to Thea and Trey, "She's been teaching me about my powers, helping me figure out what level I am."

Trey speaks for the first time, "And what level are you?"

Thea smiles, "You really have to ask Trey? He's the one they've been looking for. Can't you sense it?"

He looks at his sister, uncertain. "Why would you think that?"

"I told you things felt different with him when we reconnected. He changed somehow, and every time we see him, the pull I feel is stronger."

"That doesn't mean-"

Thea cuts her brother off with a severe look. "I can feel it, Trey. I don't know how to explain it. We distanced ourselves for a reason and we walked back into his life when we felt the change. You felt it too, don't lie." She looks in my direction before continuing, "We weren't sure if it was coming from you or not but if I'm being a hundred percent honest I didn't much care either way. I missed you and wanted us to be in each other's lives again." Looking at Trey she sighs, "So I convinced you and we made things right and just in time for the final showdown it seems." She looks over at my mother, "So you were in there with our mother?"

She nods.

"Did you escape together?"

"No. I got out first, but I heard rumors that she got escaped shortly after I did. I tried finding her, but I had no luck. She was as good at covering her tracks as I was."

Thea looks back at me. "Crazy how all this time we've grown up together and never knew the truth."

"At least you grew up knowing you were different. I just figured it out." I mumble.

"Your mom did the right thing, Will. I would have given anything for a normal childhood, but our mother was afraid they would come for us, and she wanted us prepared."

Trey shifts in his seat. "We are stronger for knowing, but it's a good thing for us that Will has always been a quick study."

Thea giggles lightly, "You always hated how easy it was for him, and now you're praising him for it. I'll never understand the opposite sex," she looks at Sage with a smile before turning her eyes on me, "I knew when you mentioned your nightmares last year that something might be going on, but I knew sixteen was a bit old to start manifesting your powers, so I thought I was wrong."

"Is that why you always asked about my dreams?"

Her cheeks flush, "Yes and no. I wanted to keep tabs on them because of the increase in the pull I was feeling towards you, but I was also worried about you. I wanted to make sure you were OK."

Sage stands abruptly, causing everyone to look in her direction.

"As great as all this is and as happy as I am for you all, we really should be talking strategy." She looks at my mother, "maybe we should all head to that school. You did say it was warded."

My mother nods. "I do think that is the best option right now. Morpheus knows about Will, and it's only a matter of time before they lock onto our location and being in the school will protect everyone's mind from him and the Company. It's the best defense we have until we are ready to take the fight to them."

"We can't just run away with our tails between our legs." Trey groans.

"I agree," I say with conviction.

"Will, be reasonable." Sage's voice is full of fear, "there are too many of us for you to take into the dreamscape. You're not strong enough yet. This is our safest bet, at least until we all have more time to train. The Company isn't something you want to go up against unprepared. Right now, we wouldn't last ten minutes against them, and then we would either be dead or back under their control and in cages."

My mother stands, drawing our attention back to her. "Sage is right. Thea, Trey, head back home and tell your parents everything, and then I want you all to pack whatever can fit in your cars and meet us here tomorrow night. We should leave as soon as possible. It will take a few days to reach the school."

"Mom."

Her eyes blaze as they fall on me. "Don't 'Mom' me. Will, I am your mother, and I couldn't protect your brother, but I'll be damned if I let anything happen to you. For once in your life, please listen to me."

Her words broke any fight I had left. I nod as Thea and Trey say their goodbyes and head out the front door. Sage follows their lead but not before giving me an apologetic look.

"Mom, I-"

"Please, Will. I don't want to argue anymore about this. You may have run across these people in your dreams, but you don't know what they are like, not really. I'm only one person, and I can't protect you from them. Not here. We need to go and not only for your safety, but for everyone's. So please, go pack what you need and then we can have dinner and hopefully have a peaceful last night in our home."

Before I can say another word, she disappears down the hall, leaving me standing alone with my thoughts. Too much has happened in the last few weeks, and I can't wrap my head around any of it. This feels like a dream. My life no longer feels real. My brother is dead. My father is gone and working for the people hunting me. I'm a freak that a mad man wants to possess so he can come back to life and go back to killing people, and God only knows what else. I have feelings for a girl who may be working both sides, and not only has my mother been hiding who I really am for my whole life, but she's just like me, and so are my best friends. Everyone I've known my whole life is different. No one is who I thought they were, and I don't know how to deal with that.

I know my mother and Sage are right, and it would be suicide to stay here, but the thought of leaving home and running away doesn't sit right with me. I was always taught to stand my ground and fight for what's right, but this feels like the opposite of that. Then again, if we stay and we lose, the bad guys win, and the world as we know it will cease to exist, and I would be the cause of it all.

I sigh as I plop myself down on the couch and rest my head in my hands.

"What am I supposed to do?"

I'm not strong enough to handle this.

I need someone to tell me what to do.

Not my mother.

Not Sage.

And not my friends.

I lift my head, knowing what I need to do, who I need to see.

I jump up from the couch and head towards my room, almost colliding with my mother in the process.

"Will, I want to give these to you."

She hands me a box.

"What is this?"

"It's everything I have on the Company along with everything you need to get to the school. Everything you could need and everything I know about our powers and family history is in this box."

"Why are you giving this to me?"

She places her hands on my wrists with a smile. "It's just in case."

I take a step back, pushing the box towards her, "No. I don't want it. Nothing is going to happen to you. Take it back."

"Will. We don't know what will happen or when. I need to know that no matter what, you are safe." She places her hand on my cheek, "you have always been the heart of this family. I loved your father and brother very much, but you gave my life purpose." She lowers her hand back to her side. "I knew I was pregnant with you before I even took a test, and I knew you were special. You came along at a dark time in my life. I needed your light, and it's because of you this family made it as far as it did."

"Mom, West is dead, and Dad abandoned us. You and I are all that is left of this family, and I'm not losing you. End of discussion."

"If I can be by your side through this, I will, but at the end of the day, if it comes to you or me, I will choose you every time."

"Mom, please stop. I don't want to have this conversation. Nothing is going to happen to either of us. We are going to the school like you wanted, and I will train and get stronger, and then I will take down the Company, and our lives will be our own for the first time. I promise you I will get us through this."

Her smile creates a calm within me.

"I know you will. I don't doubt you. I know you are meant for greatness. You will stop him. I do not doubt that, Will. However, I can't promise I'll be there to see it."

I slam the box down on the counter before my fingers run through my hair, and I pull on it in frustration.

"Stop saying that, Mom. Don't you know I can't do this without you?"

Closing the distance between us she sighs. "Will, I've been keeping something from you, and I feel it's time I tell you."

"What else could you possibly be keeping from me?"

My words cause her to flinch and immediately I wish I would take them back.

"It seems the experiments the Company did give different abilities to some of us as well as our children. I've been known to have dreams that are a foreshadowings of the future."

I stare at her, lost in her words. "What do you mean?"

"As I said, I knew you were special and would do great things because I dreamt about it more than once. The same thing about your brother. I told him to be careful, I told him he would die, but he wouldn't leave your side. I knew they would come for you and the dream always ended one of two ways. One was they took you, and we never saw you again, and then the world turned dark, the other always ended with your brother's death. He knew being there would cost him his life, but he chose it."

"Losing West almost killed me, but I can't lose you. You said I was always the heart of this family, but the truth is you're my heart. Without you, I cease to exist. I don't want to live in a world you're not in."

She places her hand on my cheek as tears stream down my face, "Will, wake up, sweety."

I look at her confused, and that's when I feel the heavyweight pulling me to the ground as my breath gets caught in my chest. My eyes fly open to see my mother hovering over me. I sit up slowly, confused.

"What happened?" I ask.

"I went into the bedroom to start packing and came out to find you unconscious on the floor. Are you feeling OK?"

I don't answer her. Instead, I pull her close to me in a crushing force.

"Will, what's wrong?"

"I had the most insane dream."

She pulls back, looking me in the eyes, "What was it about?"

"I'm not sure. You told me how you have these dreams of the future, and you knew about West possibly dying, that he knew it was either he died, or they took me, but he never left me even though he knew it would cost him his life in the end."

Her eyes shine, and for a minute, I think I see sadness in them before they change.

"Let's get you something to drink. Then, I'll help you pack, and we can eat and call it an early night. How does that sound?"

She turns away from me, heading towards the kitchen before I can reply.

It was only a dream.

If that's true, why can't I shake this horrible feeling in my chest?

Chapter 17

I lie awake in my bed for hours before sleep finally takes hold. For the first time in a long time, I had a dreamless sleep, and I couldn't be more grateful. Last night's episode really did a number on me. It felt so real, and there's something about it I can't shake. I feel like there's something I'm going to do in the near future that will cost me my mother, in some way, shape, or form.

I don't know how to explain it, but I feel her loss already heavy on my heart. Something is going to happen; I can sense it. The only thing I know for sure is I will do anything to prevent it from happening, even make a deal with the devil himself if that's what it takes.

* * *

Darkness engulfs me as thoughts of oblivion fill my mind. Something is about to change, and with it, my life will shatter in a way I've never experienced. I can't put my finger on it, but my mind is being taken over by this feeling. I feel the dread seeping into my bones. Something is terribly wrong.

"Will."

I turn towards the sound of my name, heart pounding in my chest. My eyes lock on the person responsible for my heart working double time.

"West?"

Out of the shadows, my brother moves forward, a grin plastered along his young face.

"Hey, little brother. I knew you'd find me."

He takes another step forward, slowly. This gives me time to give him a once-over. Our mother's eyes are a sweet lime green, welcoming and loving. Our father's eyes were dark deep black pits. I guess I took after my mother as my sapphire eyes resemble her more than our father and West, taking after our dad, his are just as deep and dark.

I stare at him, searching for any change, even something simple, but I find he looks the same as he did the day he was taken from us. His ear-length chocolate hair curled lightly at the ends, he closes the last foot between us, close enough to remind me of our inch difference in height as his deep dark eyes look down into mine.

"How?" I mumble.

Slapping a firm hand on my shoulder, his smile widens. "We have a lot to talk about."

I throw my arms around him, pulling him forward until we fall into our standard brotherly embrace.

I mumble into his ear, "I've missed you."

"I've always been here. I never left you."

I'm about to pull away when my body becomes heavy. If it weren't for West, I would have ended up on the ground. I can't speak as the darkness moves in around me, clouding my vision as my mind is pulled from my body.

* * *

"Will, I think we should head home. It's getting late, and you know how Mom gets when we get home after dark." West chuckles.

I smile back at him. "Yeah, she is a worry wart, that's for sure."

"Can you blame her, though?"

"I guess not."

The TV has been on every day in our house as our father watches the news. Reports of families disappearing without a trace have been the story for the last few months. Every mention of the families sets our mother more on edge. I understand her worry, but I can't help but want answers. Where did those people go? Could they have just up and moved and didn't let anyone know? I know it's unlikely, but I don't understand how an entire family could just be taken without anyone seeing it happen. One, maybe, but three? Something was wrong.

"What are you thinking about?"

West's question pulls me from my thoughts.

"Nothing much."

He closes the gap between us, moving to my side. "You know you can talk to me about anything, right?"

"I know. I just don't understand how those people could disappear without anyone seeing them. One person being taken could, maybe, that could go unnoticed, but two of those three families had four members. How could someone break into their homes and take them without anyone seeing it happen? It doesn't add up."

"It's not our job to figure it out. Leave it to the police."

I sigh. "I know. It just sucks because now we have to be home before nightfall, and our mother is up in arms living in fear. Things changed so fast around here." I turn my eyes to him, "Don't you want answers?"

West's expression tells me there's something he knows that he's not sharing with me. Growing up together, there's nothing we don't know about each other. It's an awesome thing to have a sibling. Someone to share everything with and grow together. There's always one person by your side through everything. I couldn't imagine my life without him.

I'm about to ask him what's going on in his mind when he throws an arm out in front of me, stopping me dead. I glance in his direction to see his eyes traveling the forest strip in front of us, which is the quickest way home.

"Will."

He whispers my name, but the emotion behind it tells me he's worried about something.

"I need you to run."

"What?" I say quietly as confusion fills my mind.

What could have him so on edge?

I've never seen my brother look like this, and I feel it awaken something profound inside me that's long been asleep.

His eyes flash to mine. "Will, run now!"

He pushes me lightly, turning us around but not before I catch sight of a group of strangely dressed men emerging from the forest line. My breath catches in my chest as I turn my head away from them, throwing one foot in front of the other.

"Keep going. Head straight for home. Don't stop!"

I do as he says, but only because I hear his footsteps right behind me.

Then something else crosses my mind.

What if we do go home?

What if that's what these men want?

The people that disappeared vanished from their homes as a family.

I feel myself slow down and West's hands land on my back, hard, pushing me forward once more.

"What are you doing? Keep going."

I don't slow down this time, but I say loud enough for West to hear from behind me, "We can't go home."

"What are you talking about?"

"That's what they want. The families all disappeared inside their homes. If we go back." I pant.

"Then they get us all." He gasps. "You're right. So here's what we are going to do. We need to split up."

I look over my shoulder at him. "We can't."

"We have to. It's the only way. When I say go left, there is that spot, the ditch near that house we used to play at. We will hide there and see if we can wait this out."

His words come in between deep pants.

We put a little more distance between our assailants and us before the house West is talking about comes into view, and it's time to turn left. I grab West by the shirt pulling him in the direction with me. I can't take the chance he will run off because I know that's what he's thinking of doing.

As my older brother, he's always played the role perfectly. Being there in every way a younger brother could ever need. A friend, someone to talk to, he taught me everything he knows and, most of all, always did everything in his power to keep me safe. So, I know this situation is no different, and I have a horrible feeling bubbling inside of me. I know if we separate, I'll never see him again.

We make it to the house, and I dive into the ditch, moving as far back as possible. West follows in behind me. The only thing I hear is our deep breathing. Thankful for a moment to catch my breath, I look at my brother as tension fills out his muscles.

"West."

"Will. You need to get home and let Mom and Dad know what's going on."

"They already know about these psychos."

"That's not what I'm talking about."

I feel my eyebrows meet.

"You're going to have to fill me in then."

"There's something you don't know. Something we've all been keeping from you. We wanted to keep you safe and give you a normal life for as long as we could."

"What are you talking about?"

West turns his eyes on me for the first time since we made it to safety.

"Those men, the families that went missing. They aren't exactly human."

I laugh but quickly choke on the noise, silencing myself again.

"Not human? Come on, man. Now isn't the time for one of your pranks."

His eyes become intense, and I know all joking is aside.

"I'm telling you the truth. These men are collecting people like us."

"Us?"

I feel the floodgate closing tightly around me. I can't breathe as my vision becomes spotty.

What is he talking about?

Not human.

They are collecting people like us.

Us.

"What are we?" I whisper.

"The term is Dream Walkers."

I shake my head. "I don't know what that means."

"I know. Mom will tell you everything. Trust no one else but her, do you hear me?"

I'm lost in my mind as the world around me closes in. I can't make out anything else West is saying.

West grabs me up and shakes me lightly. "Will. I need you to snap out of it."

"I'm dreaming. I have to be. Nothing you're saying is making sense."

"I know, and I'm sorry we kept the truth from you for so long, but you'll understand why soon enough. But for now, I need you to get yourself home."

The world around me snaps back into place.

"What about you?"

He smiles at me sadly. "I need to draw their attention."

"NO. Don't be crazy. We can both make it. We can sit here for a little while and then make a run for it."

"And chance we lead them home."

He's right. But there has to be a way out of this. West is a big, strong guy, and I'm not too bad.

"We can take them."

West's smile tells me he wishes it was true.

I know we can't take on that many full-grown men, but I can't leave my brother. Not to these people. I would never be able to forgive myself.

West places a hand on each shoulder. "Will, you need to make it out of this. These people, they have been searching for you. You're the one they want, not me, not those families. If they get you, everything is lost. Do you understand what I'm saying?"

I glance into his eyes, seeing defeat and sadness in them.

"You want me to leave you."

He nods.

"I can't do that, West. I can't-"

"You need to. I'm only going to distract them long enough for you to get away. Once I know you're good, I'll lose them and head home myself."

"But what if."

"I'll find you, Will, I promise."

Defeated, I know I have no choice. Once West has made up his mind, there's no stopping him, and when it comes to protecting his family, forget about it. But I know I can't just walk away.

"West, I."

Before I can say another word, I feel a sharp pain on the side of my head as the world turns dark. The last thing I see is my brother looking over me sadly.

"I'm sorry, little brother. This is the only way." He whispers.

And then the world swallows me whole.

* * *

"Will!"

West's concerned voice pulls me back from the suppressed memory.

I feel my body convulsing as the memory comes back. I woke up to darkness. I looked everywhere for my brother but with no luck. By the time I made it home, it was after 10:00 p.m., and my mother was a ball of nervous energy with tear-soaked cheeks. She flew from the couch and wrapped me in her arms when I walked through the front door. I don't remember much other than West had been found. More like his body. Someone saw it by the river and called the police. Officer Renald grew up with our mother and knew it was West. From what I heard, his face was beaten in, and his body mangled. But that wasn't what killed him, and neither was the stab wound to his abdomen. They told us he drowned.

West, the strong one.

West, the athlete.

West, the perfect swimmer, had drowned.

My brother was taken from me forever, and yet...

I forgot.

How could I forget?

I want to yell at him and ask him so many things, but my mind is slipping into oblivion again. I'm being devoured, and nothing, not even my brother's arms holding me up, can stop the pending doom as it fills my body.

Something is wrong.

I need to fight this.

I know I need to stop my mind.

Stop what I'm doing before it's too late.

This is the moment when my life will be shattered, never the same again. The moment I will chart a new course for myself and everyone around me. The moment loss will become a crippling madness.

"Will, STOP! You need to stop, NOW! WILL NO!"

West's words are lost as I slip further into the void, lost, empty, and alone.

Chapter 18

I wake up to the morning light seeping in through my curtains. Sweat covering every inch of my body, I throw off my blankets. My heart and head pounding loudly inside my aching body. I sit up faster than I should, causing the room around me to spin violently in its place. The uneasiness in my stomach bubbles up, and I know it's coming. Ignoring the throbbing mess I am, I jump from my bed, making it to the trash can with not a second to spare. I do my best to stay calm and breathe through my nose as my dinner resurfaces. My ribs scream in protest as I heave again.

And again.

And for good measure, I keep going.

In the distance, I hear light footsteps and someone's soft voice.

It can only be my mother, but I can't hear anything she's saying. I feel her cool hands on my bare shoulders. My white tank top soaked through offers no protection from the cold. My body on fire as a chill runs over my body.

Am I getting sick?

I never get sick.

"Will. What can I do?"

I breathe in slowly before mumbling. "I'm OK."

"You sure?"

"Yeah. Maybe a cup of room temp water would be good, though."

She smiles at me sadly. "You got it."

She places a kiss on my sticky forehead before heading out my door. I try to remember my dream, but it's fuzzy at best. I focus harder, knowing there's something important that I'm missing. I see the edges of the memory forming. Before I can get the bigger picture, I hear a loud crash from the direction my mother went in.

"Mom," I yell in a groggy voice.

My throat and body throbbing, I move shakingly into a standing position.

Still no answer from my mom. My heart sinks as I move as fast as my body will allow until I see a plastic bottle on the floor with water all around it. My chest tightens as fear threatens to send me over the edge. I'm about to call for her again. When I make it to the end of the hall, her figure comes into view. She's sheet white, her eyes wide like she's seen a ghost as her hand rests over her mouth. She's unmoving.

I take a slow step in her direction.

"Mom?"

Her eyes glued in the direction of the living room. I turn my body to find what has her in such a dire state. Before I turn completely around, I hear his voice.

"Hey, little brother."

"West?"

My eyes lock on his as he moves closer to us.

"How…" I ask, confused and lost for words.

"I told you, you were different." He says with a broken smile.

He isn't too happy about this situation, but I can't be bothered with that right now. Right now, my mind is frozen, thinking only one thing.

Am I dreaming?

My mother moves next to me. Without looking in my direction, she mumbles, "Will, what did you do?"

West locks eyes with our mother before speaking. "He brought me back."

She moves in until she can reach out and touch him. "Is this real?"

"Yes. I'm really here, Mom."

Her broken cries fill the room as she falls into my brother's arms. I watch from the outside, feeling like an outcast in my own home and feeling like I'm intruding in someone else's life. After all, the dead can't come back from the dead. They can't; it's physically impossible. I know Sage told me it was one

148

of my gifts and that I even entertained the idea of finding West and bringing him home, but I never thought it was possible.

I never thought I would be standing here looking at my brother alive and breathing again. As I watch them, a cold chill runs through my body, sending the fear and uneasiness surfacing once more.

Something is wrong.

Something's changed.

Magic always comes with a price.

I hear the words whispered in my ear like a caress, and I remember Sage and mine's conversation not too long ago.

"What have I done?" I say so low that no one but me hears it.

I now have no doubt that the dream with my mother telling me I was about to do something and she wouldn't be here much longer wasn't a dream at all. It was a warning, and I'm afraid that what I've just done will cause me to lose her.

I turn away from the family reunion, making my way back into my room. I find my phone, and without thinking, I open the text bar writing out the message.

West is alive.

I select three names and hit send; Thea is the first to message me back.

What?

Then Trey's message follows.

Are you sure?

Sage's text almost brings me to my knees.

Walker, tell me you didn't do what I think you did.

I close my eyes, clearing my mind before texting back the same message to everyone.

Finish packing and then come over. We might have to leave sooner than planned.

I discard my phone, not caring about anyone's reply, as I sink back onto my bed, putting my head in my hands. How could I be so reckless? I know I still have a lot to learn about my powers, and it's not like I meant to do it. I couldn't think when my memory came back from that day. I tried to ground myself, and I couldn't.

Maybe that's how I control the more immense powers? I need to feel completely taken over by something, overwhelmed. Well, what's done is done, and I can't change it. All I can do now is hope to learn how to control this power better and pray that the cost of this isn't my mother.

"West." My mother's soft voice comes from my doorway.

I lift my head from my hands and find my mother in the doorway with West. She's holding onto his hand for dear life, and I can't say I blame her. After all, this shouldn't be possible. Dead is dead. There is no coming back from it. Well, unless you're Lazarus or Jesus, but other than that, it's just not possible.

What have they done to me?

What was in that serum they injected into our parents?

How dare they play with our lives and play God.

I had no choice in becoming this. I didn't ask for it. But maybe, just maybe, I can do some good with what I've been given. I know I need to try at least. This plague has covered the world long enough, and if I don't try to stop it, who will?

Chapter 19

"When do we leave?" Thea's mother, Rose, askes my mother, Teresa.

"I would like to leave before the sun rises."

I make my way down the hallway, hearing their conversation continue in hushed tones behind me. My body is full of nervous energy. Leaving my home should bother me more than it is, but I have more important things to focus on, like Morpheus and the Company, keeping everyone here and the rest of the world safe and most of all, my growing powers. I don't know how to control them, but more than that, I don't know what I'm capable of, which creates a whole new kind of fear.

"Will."

I turn to see Thea in my doorway.

"Are you OK?" She whispers.

I rub my forehead, trying to clear my mind, closing my eyes.

"Honestly? I don't know."

She moves into my room slowly. "What can I do?"

I turn in her direction before sitting on my bed with a flop. "I don't think there is anything anyone can do."

Closing the distance between us, she drops to her knees, placing her hands on my knees. I see the love of our lifelong friendship mixed with a world of hurt in her eyes. I know, on some level, I should feel betrayed in more ways than one. Not only did my two best friends walk away from me when I needed them most, but it turns out they were lying to me all these years. I didn't know what I was, but this whole time they knew who they were, and they never told me. It's not a tiny secret, but being like family, I thought they would have told me. I know I would have told them. I planned on it. So, why didn't they tell me? We never kept anything from each other, and I was always into the weird and supernatural, so why not say something?

"Thea?"

"Yes."

"Why didn't you tell me?"

From the look in her eyes, I can tell that she knows what I'm asking about. We've known each other so long it doesn't take much to understand what the other is thinking. Thank God for that.

"I wanted to."

"But you didn't."

I move slightly, causing her hands to fall away from my knees and look at me, begging me to understand. I want to, I'm trying to, but I can't help but be angry. Everyone in my life kept me in the dark. They all lied to me, and not about what kind of milk they bought for the coffee. This was something big. Huge. And everyone lied.

How am I supposed to get over that?

How can I trust them again?

I should have known who I was, who my family and friends were, years ago. I could have been ready, prepared for the hell that has unleashed in my life. I would have been able to protect myself better, and everyone around me, had I been told.

"Will, please try and understand. This isn't something I chose for my life. It was forced upon me just like you and everyone else here. I wanted to tell you, but I knew I would be putting you in even more danger if I did. Part of me wanted to walk away from you a long time ago because I knew we were being hunted, and I wanted you to be safe from something you couldn't protect yourself from. Then when your brother died, Trey and I knew we had to."

"What do you mean you had to?"

"The disappearances and then the way West died, we knew the Company was closing in, and you had already lost your brother, and we didn't want to chance something happening to you. So, we separated ourselves from you."

"But then you came back. Why?"

She moves into a standing position.

"We heard about the ultimate walker being someone in our school. At first, we thought it was Sage. We knew there would be a new kid in school before it began, but something didn't register, so I dug deeper. We learned the walker was a male almost eighteen years old. He lived in New Jersey his whole life. Then when we heard other small things they knew about who the ultimate walker was, everything made sense. We were pretty sure it was you but didn't want to say anything until we were sure."

My mind is spinning.

"But, West is back now. That's good news, right?"

"Of course, I would do anything for my brother."

"But."

Sometimes I hate how well we know each other.

"But I can't help but feel like something is off."

"With him?"

"No. With the situation." My eyes lock with hers, "I feel like something bad is about to happen."

Thea takes a seat next to me on the bed, placing her hand back on my knee.

"One thing I've learned over the years of being your friend is when you have a bad feeling, you're normally right. So, what you need to do is focus on that feeling and see what it's telling you. Maybe you can figure out what's going to happen before it does, and we can stop it."

I shake my head lightly, "I don't think this is something that can be stopped. I feel it in my gut."

Time stands still as we sit on my bed in silence, knowing no words can stop what is coming. Thea is right about one thing. My gut feelings have never been wrong, and we would be stupid to ignore them now, so that's the last thing I'm going to do. But how do you stop something from happening when you don't know what it is? Better yet, how do you stop something that you know with every fiber of your being you can't prevent from taking place?

* * *

"I've been having a lot of intense dreams the last few weeks."

My mother and brother sit on the couch across from where I am on the floor, listening intently. I'm trying to wrap my mind around the fact that this isn't a dream. My brother is really here with us, and for now, we are a family once more. But something darker invades my thoughts as everything is telling me this moment isn't going to last much longer.

My mother leans forward, placing her elbows on her knees while folding her hands together out in front of her.

"Just say it, honey."

I nod as I feel the tears barreling to the surface.

"Last night before I saw West, I had a dream about you, Mom."

"Yes. I remember. You were acting very…nervous."

"I had a dream of you telling me about West and that you had these dreams that sometimes came true and that if it came down to your life or mine, you would choose me."

My mother leans back against the couch once more, her lips in a tight thin line.

West looks in her direction. "It's time, Mom."

I look between them both.

Looking at West she whispers, "You're right."

West turns my attention to him when he shifts slightly in his seat.

"Mom sometimes has dreams that are some form of premonitions. What the Company did to them in there, the serum, it messed with everyone differently."

My mother nods. "For me, it was being able to manipulate the outside world, as we talked about before, and the dream premonitions. For others, it's different things, and for some, it's nothing."

I move into a standing position and lean up against the wall closest to them on the couch.

"I'm guessing in some way, maybe you have the same power. Maybe it was trying to tell you I won't be around much longer. Sometimes the message is hard to figure out. But honey, you're almost a man. You're strong and independent, and I've taught you everything I can. The rest will come, and you have your friends, the school and your brother, and I'll always be here. You can't get rid of me that easily."

I move to the spot in front of her and drop to my knees.

"I don't want them to teach me."

She places her hand on my cheek with a weak smile.

"You can't let this affect you. Morpheus will sense your weakness, and with it, he will win. Whatever comes next, we will face it together, as a family."

"Mom's right, Will. He's coming, and we need to be prepared."

I move into a standing position once more.

I walk out the door, leaving them alone, knowing if anyone can help, it's Sage.

Chapter 20

"I need your help."

"Anything." She smiles.

"My mother has these premonitions, and she thinks I might too, and if she's right, we need to stop the next one from coming to pass."

Her face becomes uneasy as her forehead creases.

"I don't know how I can help with that."

"There has to be something. You know more than anyone else here, and you know about the herbs and protection wards. Isn't there some kind of protection potion or something we can use to counteract it or change what's coming? Something to use to protect everyone from Morpheus?"

I know I'm grasping at straws, but right now, I don't care. I'll take anything, and if my mother doesn't see a way, the only other person who might is Sage.

Sage places her hand gently on mine. "Will, what did you see? What are we trying to stop?"

My eyes connect with hers as fear sinks its nails deep into my flesh. I know saying the following words will make the reality before me more real in my mind, and I don't think I'm ready for that. But I know if my mother stands a chance, I need to tell Sage everything I know, and maybe, just maybe, she will have a way for us to defeat this.

"Since I brought back West, I don't know. I just have this feeling in the pit of my stomach. It's telling me my mother is going to die."

Her mouth drops slightly.

"The cost." She whispers.

I nod.

"I can't make any promises, but I will try my best. Just give me a few minutes to go through what I have with me and think about what might work. But I need you to keep in mind that if something like this existed, we would have used it a long time ago, so don't get your hopes up."

"Thank you," I whisper.

"What are friends for?" She smiles shyly.

Without thinking, I lean down and kiss her on the cheek, causing us to blush.

"I was also thinking of maybe going into your mind and seeing what happened to you when the Company had you. Maybe they made you forget something that could be helpful."

"Sure. That's a good idea. Let's get through this, and then we can try that."

I smile before turning away from her and heading for the kitchen. It's around seven o'clock at night now, but no one has had anything to eat. I pull some kidney beans and mac and cheese from the cabinet and chicken from the fridge and go to work. An hour later, we are all sitting around the house eating our meal.

"Thank you, Will. This is delicious." Rose, Thea and Trey's mother, says with a bright smile.

With their mouths currently full of food, everyone smiles and nods in agreement in our direction.

"I figured we should eat before sleeping for a few hours. The journey to the school isn't close from what my Mom said. I also prepared some sandwiches for everyone while we are on the road and have drinks and snacks together for when we are ready to head out."

Rose turns in the direction of my mother, smiling from ear to ear.

"You raised him well. He will make a fine husband one day."

Her words send my heart into overdrive.

Husband.

I'm not even eighteen yet.

Although her words made me a bit uneasy, seeing the smile on my mother's face made me realize it was more for her benefit. My actions show that she has done her best for the last almost eighteen years. She has been the best mother and taught me everything that matters. Rose is right. My mother molded me into the person I am today. Everything I am is because of her. What would I be without her?

Sage walks up behind me, pulling me from my thoughts.

"I think I might have something." She whispers.

I nod my head and excuse myself from the table, following Sage into my bedroom. My bed is a mess, covered in herbs, paperwork, and stones of all kinds.

"You've been busy," I say with a smile.

"I wanted to check everything before jumping into it. I think I've found something that should work. There's still a chance it won't, but I'm fairly certain it will. I read about how our powers were told to come from witches and that witch blood runs inside us. It's how we can do the things we can do. We are a form of witches, but some of us have stronger connections to the power than others, and I have no doubt your family is one of them."

She picks something up off the bed and hands it to me.

"This is a magic talisman. I stole it from the Company before they let me go and told me to find you. I read that it belonged to one of the strongest witches over a hundred years ago. Morpheus killed her and took this as a trophy, but I don't think he really knew what it was."

"What is it?"

"It's many things, but one is a protection amulet. According to what I read, it's the strongest ever to be made by a witch. Her line was wiped out when he killed her, but, leading up to her, there was no one stronger than her family. She made all kinds of things for other witches, but this one she kept for herself."

"Why?"

"Because its power is the strongest, and it's capable of doing more than just protecting the owner, but we can get into that another time."

"You think it's strong enough to protect my mother?"

"If this doesn't work, I don't think anything will. With this, she at least has a chance."

I look down at the object in my hand, and the first thing I notice is how old it looks. The chain is made of a thick brown rope, and at its center are five small stones, all different in color. They have a piece of string in between each one to separate them. The five stones run from deep blue to light purple.

"Thank you, Sage."

"I really hope it works."

My eyes find hers.

"Me too."

I take the amulet and head into the living room to find my mother and brother still sitting in the same place I left them. My right hand begins to tingle the closer I get to her. Almost like the amulet's magic is surging.

"Sage thinks she's found something," I say before putting my hand out in front of me to reveal our only hope.

"Is that?" West mumbles.

My mother scoots forward on the couch, her mouth open slightly.

"It can't be. I've heard rumors about it from the school, but we all thought it was a superstition."

My eyebrows reach my hairline.

"What are you two talking about?"

My mother's eyes lock with mine, but it's my brother who speaks first.

"Mom used to tell me about where our magic came from and about our great great great...well, you get the point. She was our great grandmother, and she was the strongest witch known in existence. Everyone knew about her."

"Wait, I thought Morpheus killed her and put an end to her line?" I ask confused.

I hear Sage and the others move in behind me to listen to the story.

My mother smiles before continuing. "He did kill her, but what he didn't know was she already had a child. A daughter. So her name was lost over time since women rarely keep their last name once married. No one knew. They all believed her line ended with her."

"How do you know for sure she did have a child and that we are her descendants?" I ask.

My mother's smile grows wider.

"My family had their suspicions, and they ran every test there was to link us back to her. Once we learned the truth, we had our person on the inside at the Company switch out all our blood and other tests they had taken. We knew if they weren't destroyed that Morpheus would learn the truth, and we would all be in danger."

"Why did he kill her?" Thea asks from behind me.

"She caught onto him and what he was doing and was gathering all the other covens to trap him."

"In the dreamscape." I mumble.

My mother nods.

"Yes. But he killed her before the plan worked. It wasn't for another three years before he was stopped."

"So, you're telling me we are connected to this witch?"

She nods.

Trey's voice silences me, "Well, mind blown."

Everyone turns to look in his direction as Thea rolls her eyes at him, causing everyone to laugh. I turn my attention back to my mother as she takes the amulet from my hand, but the feeling it created when in my possession still lingers.

"If anything will work, this would be it, Will. How did you get this?"

I turn to Sage. "She stole it from the Company before she left."

My mother's gaze moves past me to land on Sage.

"Thank you."

Sage smiles, but I can see she's nervous. I've never seen this side of her. She's usually full of backbone and sometimes, even scary. I laugh internally at my thoughts. My mother places the necklace around her neck before turning to everyone in the room.

"I think we should all try to get a few hours of sleep. We will get up around one, pack up the cars, and leave while it's still dark out. The trip will take about three days."

Everyone nods before heading to their designated sleeping zones we had picked out when everyone first arrived. Despite finding this amulet, I still can't shake the crippling feeling inside.

"Will, can I talk to you?" My mother's voice sounds sad.

I turn around to see her eyes carry the same sadness as her voice. I nod as West slaps me on the back and exits the room. She gestures for me to take the empty seat next to her.

"Will, I want you to know how very proud of you I am. Rose was right earlier in her statement. You have turned into a fine young man, and soon you will be a legal adult." Her smile widens across her face, "Eighteen. I can't believe it. It feels like only yesterday I brought you home from the hospital and was changing your diapers."

"Ugh Mom, please."

Laughing lightly, she continues, "Sorry. It's just, you've become everything I ever thought you would be and then some. I know you will be the one to put an end to Morpheus."

I look down at my hands. "How can you be so sure?"

She places her hand on my knee. "Because I know you. He doesn't stand a chance. You have always put others before yourself and done what's right. I know you will make the right decisions."

"I hope so. Sometimes I think you have too much faith in me."

Placing her hand lightly on my cheek, she mumbles, "Never."

I can see her faith in me in her eyes. I hope she's right. I've seen how strong I am, strong enough to scare me, but I still wonder if it will be enough to stop him. Learning we are descendants of the most powerful witch only makes me wonder what else I'm capable of. The one thing I do know for sure is no matter the cost, I can't let Morpheus take over my body. If he does, no one will stand a chance. I've only had a taste of what I can do, and these gifts in the wrong hands, in his hands, would be catastrophic.

"I'll do my best."

"Your best is always enough, don't ever doubt that. You have made my life full in every way, Will. You are a gift to everyone around you, and even though you can't see it yet, you are a born leader."

I chuckle, "I think you have the wrong son."

"Nope."

We laugh together and then sit in silence for a few moments before we head to our room, ready for a few hours of hopefully peaceful dreams. She stops in her doorway, looking at me. Love fills her eyes, a love I've become so used to seeing from her. A love that has filled me and helped me become the man I am today. A love I can't live without. A smile forms on her face before we say our goodnights and she disappears behind her door.

* * *

"Oh, the young walker finally returns," Morpheus says from the darkness.

"I have nothing to say to you."

I just have to wait out this nightmare, and I'll be back home and on my way to someplace where hopefully they can teach me how to lock this maniac out of my mind.

"I think you'll be interested in what I have to say." His tone is sinister and playful.

"I doubt it."

His monstrous laugh fills the air around me, "Oh, so you don't care that as we speak, your mother is slipping into the afterlife? And all because of you."

I stop breathing at his words as my saliva becomes lodged in my throat.

"What are you talking about?"

"Don't play dumb. It doesn't suit you."

Anger boils over as I run toward his voice and grip him up, pulling his face mere inches from mine.

I snarl. "Tell me."

His smile sends a chill through my body. "I'll do one better." He places his hands on my forearms, "I'll show you."

The last thing I see is the laughter in his eyes before my vision turns and I'm back home. I look around until my mother comes into view. She's in the kitchen grabbing something to drink.

She looks fine.

She makes her way down the hall back to her room, but something isn't right. She stops mid-stride as her glass falls to the floor, sending its contents in every direction. My mother's hands move to her chest, and I can see she's having a hard time breathing as her eyes roll up into her head and she drops to her knees.

"Mom!"

One hand is now on the wall as she tries to hold herself up. I see the panic and fear in her eyes as she looks in the direction where I'm standing, right in front of my bedroom door. Her eyes are pleading, and I know time is running out. She struggles to try to stand. I try to move towards her, but I'm stuck in place. Angry, I push against the invisible force holding me in place, but it's no use.

I look back at my mother, who is now crawling toward my room. Her eyes are glassy as she stops once more and sinks to the floor. She looks in my direction as she struggles to speak.

"I'm sorry, Will. I love you, I will always be with you."

Then her head sinks to the ground as her eyes close.

"No!"

The picture disappears, and Morpheus comes back into view.

"Like what you see?" He says happily.

My grip on him becomes forceful as I rock him back.

"What did you do?" I scream.

"Nothing. You did this, dear boy. You brought back your brother, and this is the cost."

His words send me on a roller coaster as the anger moves to the surface so fast it nearly chokes me. My body turns heavy as I fight to stay in a standing position and the scene around me begins to fade as I gasp for breath.

No, you need to stop.

"To think you're the one I've been waiting for, searching for all this time. Someone so....weak. She's nothing, no one and you lost her all for a brother." He laughs, "You have so much to learn dear boy. People come and go, but power, power is forever. Power creates fear and puts you at the top of the food chain dear boy."

I look at him angrily, "I don't see you at the top. Fear and power didn't do much for you then I suppose." I smile.

He grins trying to hide his anger and annoyance with me. "That was then and this is now. I've learned a lot while being locked away in this prison and now," his gaze falls on me sending a chill over my skin, "I have you. The strongest among us. No one can go up against me once I have you."

Through bared teeth I say, "You'll never have me."

"Oh, but I already do."

His words bring me back as I try to let go of him realizing what I'm doing, but he holds my hands in place.

"Oh, no, you don't. Not yet. We are so close."

No.

I need to move away from him. I can't do this.

Fading fast, I focus as hard as I can. It feels like an eternity passes before my hands release him, and I sink to the dirt floor at his feet.

His sinister chuckle fills the darkness around me as I sink further into oblivion. The world around me is fading fast.

"I'll be seeing you soon, boy."

* * *

I bolt into a seated position, head pounding as my heart fights to return to its normal rhythm. My limbs are like boulders, making it hard to remove myself from my bed. All I'm missing is the violent vomiting. I remember this feeling from when I brought back West, and I'm thankful the last piece is nowhere. Not only because I hate throwing up, but I knew if I were getting sick right now, it would mean I had done the one thing I refused to do.

It would mean I released him.

I sigh in relief, but it's short-lived when I remember what Morpheus showed me. I stumble, running for my door, barely able to keep upright. I throw the door open wide as it bangs against the wall moving into the hallway as I drop to my knees.

Lying on the ground in the middle of the hallways, unmoving, is my mother. Fear crippling me, I fight through it, pushing myself to make it to her side. If I can do nothing else, I need to do that.

I reach her side and fall into a heap next to her. I place my hand on her shoulder, trying to wake her.

"Mom? Mom, wake up."

I hear my voice breaking, but I push down the feeling of defeat.

She's not dead.

I move her onto her back and lower my head to her chest. I strain, trying hard to hear her heartbeat.

Nothing.

I lift my head and look at her face, placing my hand just above her nose and mouth, willing even the smallest of breaths to tickle my skin.

I wait.

And wait some more.

Nothing.

"No. No, this isn't happening." I cry out.

I grab her body, pulling it onto my lap, wrapping my arms around her, and holding her still-warm body close to mine. I don't know when I started rocking us back and forth, and I don't notice until I stop and throw my head to the sky, releasing an ear-piercing scream.

"Mom!"

I feel the tears falling down my cheeks in a waterfall motion, and I do nothing to stop them. I glance down at her unmoving body. I unconsciously remove a strand of hair away from her face.

She looks like she's sleeping.

That's it.

She's only sleeping.

"Will?" Thea's voice is quiet.

I barely hear her, but even then, I pay her no mind. My eyes see everyone at the end of the hallway looking down at my mother and me, but I ignore them. I make out my brother moving everyone aside until his eyes fall on me. His expression, sad, defeated. I shake my head violently.

"She's only sleeping," I say in a voice that doesn't sound like my own.

"Oh, Will." Sage whispers.

West moves toward me slowly. Making it to my side, he kneels in front of me, placing his hand on my shoulder.

"Will. You need to let me take her."

I shake my head violently. "No."

"Will. We need to leave. It's not safe here."

My eyes ablaze land on him. "I don't care! You know where the school is, you know how to drive. You take them. I'm staying here. I can't leave her. I won't."

"Will."

"No. Don't you see? This is all my fault." I sob.

"No. None of this is your fault, Will."

I feel the tears as they continue to wet my hot cheeks.

"Yes, it is. If I knew how to handle my powers, I never would have." I trail off.

West's eyes turn sad but understanding. "You never would have brought me back."

I glance at him in shame. "I didn't mean."

"I know." He smiles sadly. "But Will, you know what she wanted."

I close my eyes as I hold onto her tightly. "I can't, West."

"Let me help you. We aren't safe here. If we stay, we will share the same fate, and her sacrifice would have been for nothing."

I open my eyes, looking into his, seeing they match my heartbreak. I never thought I'd see the day when I had to bury my mother. Her loss is something I will carry with me the rest of my days, and all I can hope is to find a way to keep going without her. Like she asked. Like she expected of me.

I only hope I can make her proud.

My heart breaks inside my chest as my knuckles turn white and my arms start to tingle with how tightly I am holding onto her. I know West is right, and I need to let her go, but I can't.

I just can't.

Chapter 21

Morpheus

The heaviness subsides as I peel my eyes open. The transition isn't something I anticipated. The feeling of being torn apart slowly isn't a pleasant one, but I guess that's how all my conquests felt so maybe it's only fitting I should endure it at this moment. A moment I have waited so long for.

Looking down, I find unfamiliar hands. Hands that aren't my own. But they are strong. They will do just fine. I smile as I look off into the void of my life's work, knowing the fun is about to begin.

"I'm back."

Thank You For Reading

Did You Enjoy This Book

You Can Make A Difference

Reviews go a long way and help all authors but for us indie/self-published authors it's the most important as it helps our work get more notice. We self-published authors don't have the marketing others get with a publisher. However, I feel I have something better than they do.

I have committed and loyal readers that I appreciate more than anything. Without you reading and reviewing, my dream would still be only a dream, when now it's become reality. So thank you.

Honest reviews of my books help bring them to the attention of other readers.

So, if you enjoyed this book please take a moment and head over to Amazon and Goodreads and leave your honest review because they help more than you know.

About the Author

Laura Lukasavage started writing shortly after her mother's passing when she was only fourteen years old. She remembered how her mom would write poems and letters to her step dad and as a way to feel close to her mother she took up writing. She started with poems in eight grade and then short stories in high school. Once she started college in 2009 at Neumann University in Aston, PA her interest only grew. By the time she would transfer from Neumann to Rowan University in Glassboro, NJ in 2011, after her father's passing, is when she knew what her passions truly were. She majored in Radio, TV and Film productions with a minor in creative writing. She found her love of film and writing meshed together and this is where she felt at peace. Laura writes as a way to escape from reality but to also deal with life as a whole. She writes hoping that one day her books will be an escape for someone needing it just like the books she read in high school to escape the recent loss of her mother.

Also by Laura Lukasavage

See You On The Other Side

Blissfully happy, newlyweds Sam and Jane are looking forward to years of building their life together. But the reality they thought would be theirs is shattered by tragedy when Jane dies.

Now both Sam and Jane are lost in the darkness alone. Unable to see any way forward. Only by finding her way to peace can Jane help pull Sam out of the depths of his grief.

But can he be saved when the love of his life has been ripped away from him, taking the future they planned together with her?

Moonlight Secrets (Book #1)

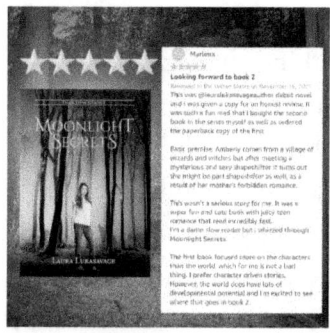

When Amberly walks into the forbidden forest, like so many times before, she doesn't expect her whole world and life to change. Having a run-in with a wolf can be a scary thing for anyone, but would you find it more terrifying if you could communicate telepathically with one? And what if you were the only one who could? What if that wolf told you there were things about your life that you didn't know? Would you take the chance and risk everything to get answers?

While dealing with her new life and all the secrets in it, Amberly is also trying to sort through the hidden feelings she has for her best friend, Logan, who might just be feeling the same. What if you had to choose between the one person who's known you your whole life and been there for you through it all, and someone who you barely know? But what if that person you barely know showed you a world you never knew anything about and woke something inside of you that made you come to life? If you had to choose, what would you do?

From having your father come back from the dead to almost dying not once but twice, there's no shortage of drama, suspense, secrets, lies, betrayal, love, and friendship in Amberly's journey.

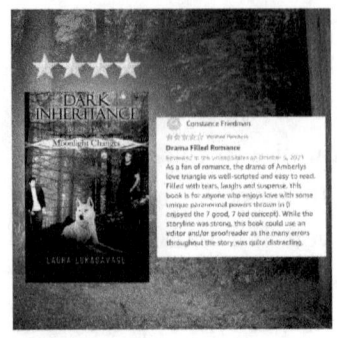

Moonlight Changes (Book #2)

Amberly's life is anything but normal. Finding out the truth behind who she really was didn't even crack the surface of all the changes coming her way. Learning she is being hunted by someone hundreds of years old is the least of her problems. Dream walking into another shape shifters mind that needs her help only adds to her troubled life. But when she starts having visions and seeing everyone, she love's dead at your feet she starts to scrabble against the clock. Wanting only to train, become stronger, so that she can protect the ones she loves from their horrible fate.But can fate be stopped?However, the new shape shifter isn't the only person she's dream walking with. She finds Vladimir's right hand, Aidan invading her mind more then once. Who is he? Why does he feel so familiar to her? While dealing with all the changes in her powers and turning eighteen, she's trying to find some stability in her life and her love life is anything but that. But catching Julian kissing the new girl is only the start to her world unraveling at the seems. How is she supposed to learn how to control her powers, learn to shift and defend herself when her heart is broken? Knowing Vladimir is coming for her and the ones she loves, she wipes away the tears and goes to work. She will do anything to make sure her vision doesn't come to pass.Don't miss the second book in the Dark Inheritance series.

Moonlight Legacy (Book #3)
Serenity:

It's all happening as I've seen in my dreams. Amberly learned who she was. Was united with those she should have known her entire life. Met her true mate.

And then was torn from us all.

But hope still springs, because in being lost, Amberly will find answers and learn the true strength of her heart.

The last battle might have been lost, but the war has only just begun. And Amberly's choices from here on will send out ripples that will shape the future of our world.

But can an eighteen year old choose the right path when darkness and grief obscures every way forward?

This is book 3 in the Dark Inheritance Series and should be read in order.

Enough Is Enough

My name is Elena and I have put a plan in motion to escape my abuser and recurring nightmare. However, there is that old saying about the best laid plans going awry...

Escaping your abuser only to have new obstacles laid out in front of you. Now not only does my body need to heal but my mind as well. Beaten, torn down and broken. I'm not longer the woman I once was and to find her again will be no easy task. Anxiety takes over my mind and body whenever any man gets too close. Even if its someone I know would never hurt me.

Can I overcome this fear? Can I get close to a man again and live out the rest of my life in peace, or am I destined to be alone and afraid for the rest of my days?

A story of a broken woman fighting to stabilize her life after ending her abuse. Can she silence the fears in her mind and allow herself a happy ending with her lifelong friend Jason, or will the anxiety and fear her husband beat into her win out?

Jim has become Elena's living nightmare but today everything changes. Elena, has put her plan in motion. A plan to take back both her life and happiness and leave the nightmares behind. Or so she hopes.

Elena is ready.
   Ready to take back her life.
   Ready to be free of the nightmare that has become her normal everyday existence.